CW00822381

1 MONTH OF
FREE
READING

at

www.ForgottenBooks.com

By purchasing this book you are eligible for one month membership to ForgottenBooks.com, giving you unlimited access to our entire collection of over 1,000,000 titles via our web site and mobile apps.

To claim your free month visit:

www.forgottenbooks.com/free793821

ISBN 978-0-483-97335-0
PIBN 10793821

This book is a reproduction of an important historical work. Forgotten Books uses
state-of-the-art technology to digitally reconstruct the work, preserving the original format
whilst repairing imperfections present in the aged copy. In rare cases, an imperfection in
the original, such as a blemish or missing page, may be replicated in our edition. We do,
however, repair the vast majority of imperfections successfully; any imperfections that
remain are intentionally left to preserve the state of such historical works.

COLLECTION

OF

BRITISH AUTHOR

TAUCHNITZ EDITION.

VOL. 1613.

FRENCH PICTURES IN ENGLISH CHALK
BY
E. C. GRENVILLE MURRAY.

IN TWO VOLUMES.
VOL. II.

FRENCH PICTURES

IN

ENGLISH CHALK.

BY

E. C. GRENVILLE MURRAY,

AUTHOR OF

"THE MEMBER FOR PARIS," "THE BOUDOIR CABAL," ETC.

COPYRIGHT EDITION.

IN TWO VOLUMES.

VOL. II.

LEIPZIG

BERNHARD TAUCHNITZ

1876.

CONTENTS

OF VOLUME II.

OUR NEW BISHOP.

(CONTINUED.)

OUR NEW BISHOP.

APROPOS OF THE "ŒCUMENICAL."

(Continued.)

IV.

The election over, an adjournment to the supper-room was voted, and the health of our bishop-designate, proposed by Madame la Marquise and seconded by Madame la Préfête, was drunk in brimmers of champagne. Certes, if many hear no good of themselves when they lay their ears next a keyhole, others, more fortunate, might reap a few hours' exquisite bliss in listening from behind a door to what is being said of them within. I fancy M. Ponceau, for instance, would have found no reason to complain had some considerate spirit lifted him by the hair of his head and deposited him privately under our supper-table. For ninety minutes or so without cease, his trumpet was bravely blown for him to the tuneful accompaniment of jingling glasses and clattering silver forks, and when, at last, we rose from table (it being then 1.30 a.m.) a motion was carried to the effect that we should set to work at once upon the petition to Government, and not separate until all the preliminaries had been concluded.

So as not to lose time, however, the drawing up of the petition was confided to M. Jules Sifflot, who sat down to the task at once, and in less than half an hour had indited an address remarkable at once for its truth, its elevation of language, and its pathetic sentiments.

I subjoin this valuable document:—

To His Excellency the Minister of Justice.

Monsieur le Ministre,

We, the undersigned inhabitants of the diocese of Ville-Rosé, respectfully approach your Excellency in the hope that the recent heavy bereavement from which we are suffering will give us a claim to your sympathies and your attention. Your Excellency is aware that the genial Christian virtues which so pre-eminently distinguished our late Bishop rendered him inexpressibly dear to his flock. His patience, his modesty; his generous solicitude for all in sorrow, and, above all, the saintly humility which characterized the whole conduct of his life, gave him a place in our hearts such as had never been held before, save by his Majesty the Emperor, her Majesty the Empress, and his Highness the Prince Imperial. Under these circumstances it is but natural, Monsieur le Ministre, that in the first flush of our profound grief we should earnestly desire that the Bishop who is to succeed to Monseigneur's place in our diocese should also be the recipient of his wealthy heritage in our affections. Well knowing, as we do, how deep is the attention, how anxious the care, and how equitable the spirit which his Majesty's Government always brings to bear upon the selection of dignitaries for the Church or State, we freely confess that we could not do better than await the appointment which it may please his Majesty's Government to make, confident that the appointment will be of a nature to satisfy our most cherished hopes and fill us with the liveliest gratitude. At the same time, should his Majesty's Government have not yet made choice of a candidate, we would most humbly venture to pray your Excellency to consider the claims of Monsieur le Chanoine Ponceau, a priest who seems to have been especially fashioned by Providence to pick up the mantle of Monseigneur Fulmine. Far be it from us to have recourse to any step which should seem to your Excellency to savour of presumption. But in the interests of truth we think it right to state that ever since the day when our late bishop left us, there has been a unanimous and heartfelt hope in the breast of every inhabitant of the diocese that the Government would select M. l'Abbé Ponceau. Children lisp the name of our beloved Canon in the streets, mothers bless him, old men pray for him; his reputation for goodness, abnegation, and charity is scarcely inferior to that of Monseigneur Fulmine. Shall we add that, like all the truly virtuous men of this land, M. Ponceau is deeply devoted to that Great Sovereign who has bestowed upon France seventeen years of uninterrupted order, and whose reign shines in the chronicles of our country with the beaming light of incomparable glory? No, your Excellency has divined this, for had it been otherwise, M. Ponceau's name would not have had the support of the undersigned petitioners, who beg to subscribe themselves, with deepest respect,

Monsieur le Ministre,

Your Excellency's most humble, faithful, and obedient Servants.

"One would think you had done nothing but write petitions to Government all your life," says the Marquise, as M. Jules Sifflot finishes the reading of his composition.

"It's the official candidate style," answers M. Sifflot modestly. "I learned it from reading Monsieur le Marquis's addresses to his constituents and Monsieur le Préfet's speeches in favour of Monsieur le Marquis. It is a good style, rich and comprehensive, and has the merit of swallowing the whole leek at once without making any bones about it."

The Prefect and the Marquis look at each other

and grin. Madame la Marquise raps M. Sifflot on the fingers; but the petition is assented to nevertheless, and the only thing that now remains to be done is to arrange about obtaining the signatures. The General promises that two hundred men out of the garrison shall sign on the morrow morning, the Prefect will see that a like number of free and independent citizens shall affix their names in the forenoon, and the Mayor engages to collect signatures from all the maimed, halt, and sick in the hospital and asylums.

"What we want now," says Madame la Générale, "is a few of the clergy. It would look well if we had the signatures of a couple óf hundred priests."

"Yes, it would," assents the Marquis; "but the only way to get them would be to convince each of the two hundred that he was petitioning in favour of himself; and that is a stroke of diplomacy which would require more time than we can spare."

"What do you say to doing this instead?" asks the Marquise. "It's an idea that has just occurred to me. Suppose we go to the Abbé Bonneau, and get him to accompany you to Paris with the petition? He is so good that he would do it willingly, and the effect produced would be excellent, for the dear man is known everywhere as a saint."

"Yes, but let us hope the Minister will appreciate

his merits better than we seem to have done," rejoins M. Jules Sifflot, laughing at the recollection of the nine blackballs.

"I am certain he will," says the Marchioness, positively. "I was talking with his Excellency one day about this very Abbé Bonneau, and he told me the old man was the very best priest in France."

"And so he is very likely," answers Madame la Préfète; "but, after all, I don't think we can be blamed for not having voted for him. He would never do for a bishop; he would give all his clothes away to the poor, and leave himself not so much as his mitre to go to church in——"

The Prefect takes out his watch. "It's getting late," he interposes; "it's already past three. Let us settle our plans at once. Madame's idea about the Abbé Bonneau is a good one. Somebody had better see him without delay."

"That can be done while you are collecting the signatures," says the Marquis; "but I think the best plan of action will be for us all to meet at the prefecture at two, after the petition has been signed. We can then go together, and call upon Canon Ponceau, to tell him what we have been doing; and after that go to the Abbé Bonneau, who can take the five o'clock train with us for Paris. If we manage things promptly, we shall be back here in thirty-six hours from this time, with M. Ponceau's appointment already signed and sealed."

This proposal was approved, and just as the first gleam of morning twilight was dawning, the guests of M. le Marquis left the Château de la Roche-Courbette, well pleased with having, as they fancied, manufactured a bishop, and promising to meet again at two.

V.

I will do the Prefect and the General this justice, that after a short hour or two's sleep, they set to work like men. The General, as soon as his breakfast was over, had two hundred rank and file marched up to his house, and explained to them, through the window, that they would have to come up, six at a time, into the vestibule, and sign a paper that was laid on the table; those who could not write would get those who could to sign for them. He added that it was about a new bishop, and asked them, for the form of the thing, whether they saw any objection. This idea tickled them so vastly, that they all began laughing together; upon which the General laughed too, and went back to take his coffee, announcing, however, before going, that any soldier who made blots should have two days in the *Salle de Police.* The Prefect, whose high position rendered it unadvisable that he should take too ostensibly prominent a part in the whole affair, deferred the task of collecting signatures to his secretary. This young gentleman, who was of an imaginative turn, forthwith went down to the lower end of the town, where some Government works were in progress, and presenting the workmen with some sheets of paper, told them laconically to write their names down; which they did, submissively, one by one, without asking questions. Fifty signatures having been obtained in this way, the secretary paid domiciliary visits to three girls' schools, where he undertook a brief panegyric of Canon Ponceau, paid a few compliments to the governesses, and obtained as many signatures as there were ladies. A hundred and ten, however, still remained to be found, and the young gentleman was beginning to feel tired. He accordingly chartered a small boy, to whom he gave a franc and a ream of foolscap, on the first page of which he wrote, in big letters, "*Votez pour Ponceau, candidat éclectique.*" "You'll go," said he to the small boy, "and get a hundred and ten workmen to sign their names on to the blank pages. If they ask who Ponceau is, you will tell them he is a cousin of M. Henri Rochefort. If they want to know what *éclectique* signifies, you will say it means good dinners."

An hour afterwards the small boy returned with three hundred names, many of which were interlarded with such appropriate exclamations as *"La Liberté ou la Mort!"* *"A bas les Tyrans!"* *"Vive la Lanterne!"* *"A Chaillot les Prêtres!"* etc., etc. The honest signers had thought that their votes were required on behalf of a "friend and brother," and had testified to the warmth of their sentiments in the usual way. "Bah!" laughed the secretary; "it doesn't much matter. Petitions sent to Ministers are always thrown into the waste-paper basket, and nobody ever thinks of looking at the signatures." And upon this he gave the small boy another franc, and walked back to the prefecture, pleased enough with his morning's work.

The Mayor, meanwhile, had been as busy as the General and the Prefect's secretary. He had gone recruiting suffrages in the charitable institutions under his control, and had obtained them as easily as he had at the last political election, when he had mustered such a fine collection of cripples to vote for the Prefect's candidate. But by this time the touting and canvassing in different quarters had begun to excite attention. Little by little the truth leaked out, and as news spreads fast in small towns, where the inhabitants have nothing to do all day but count their fingers and thumbs, it very quickly became known that the authorities were starting a petition for having Canon Ponceau appointed bishop. We then had a reproduction of that eternally instructive story of Panurge's sheep. Seeing some of their fellow-townsmen signing their names on sheets of paper, divers ambitious citizens became possessed with the desire of signing too. Many men and women who could not possibly have the smallest interest in seeing M. Ponceau elected, hurried up feverishly to add their names to the petition. As the morning advanced and the rumours waxed more persistent, quiet people left their houses and went down into the streets to ask what the matter was. The day was a lovely one, and the cathedral bells, as it happened, were ringing full volley in honour of some saint. Of course this was somehow associated with the talk about M. le Chanoine Ponceau, and there were plenty who believed that the jubilant Canon was already treating himself to an exulting peal as thanksgiving for his appointment. Gradually a crowd began to gather round the door of the Mairie, where a copy of the petition was displayed for signatures, and, before long, the police had to be called into requisition to form the gathering into a long *queue*, and only admit signers three at a time. By twelve o'clock the Mairie had received a thousand names; by one, five hundred more had been added; and at two, when the nine promoters of the petition met at the prefecture according to arrangement, the crowd had already grown enthusiastic, and were for going and giving M. le Chanoine an ovation in front of his house.

"Our idea seems to have taken root," began the Marquis as soon as we were all collected.

"And what a noise it is making!" exclaimed the Marchioness, looking out of the window in astonishment at the tumultuous assemblage below.

"Yes," says the Prefect, with evident uneasiness. "I begin to wish we had let the business alone. If the Government have already thought of some one for the appointment, they will not thank me for having got up all this uproar."

Madame la Préfête bit her lips, and looked out of the window with the Marquis. "Is there no way of stopping them?" she asked anxiously, not at all liking the idea of a quarrel between her husband and the Government.

"*Vive Madame la Préfête!*" cries an urchin in the crowd, who has perceived the two ladies.

"*Vive Rochefort!*" yelps another.

"*Ohé Lambert!*"

"*Vive Raspail! Hop! O La Lanterne!*"

"*A bas les Préfets de Ratapoil!*"

"Confound them, there they go," mutters the

Prefect, with a shrug of the shoulders. "I ought to have foreseen all this."

"Well, all we've got to do now is to breast it," observes Jules Sifflot resolutely. "I think, too, we ought to go and call on Canon Ponceau at once, for he won't be able to understand what on earth all this means."

"To be sure, we have been forgetting the Canon; he must be half out of his wits by this time," exclaims the Marquis.

"We had better all go there together," says the Prefect. "When we have seen him we will look up the Abbé Bonneau, and then go straight off to Paris. Minutes are becoming precious. By hook or crook we must get Ponceau appointed."

The ladies adjusted their bonnets, the men put on their hats, and the whole party of nine of us went down the staircase and sallied out into the Square together. With such a crowd as there was, it was impossible that we could pass unnoticed. The Prefect, the General, the Mayor, and the Marquis, were recognized immediately. The shouting and chaffing ceased. There was an exchange of salutations, a falling back right and left; and then the whole crowd, re-forming itself in our rear, followed us in silence to see where we were going. So long as we were in the market-place the quiet continued;

but when it became visible that we were making for the church precincts where the Canons lived, our escort took it as a matter of course that we were going to pay a visit of congratulation to M. Ponceau, and burst out into cheers, rare and faint at first, but growing gradually louder and more general, until they culminated into an immense and frantic roar when we finally stopped before the Canon's house.

"For Heaven's sake, M. le Préfet, what does all this mean?" stammered M. Ponceau, opening the door to us himself, and showing us into his parlour. He was very pale and agitated, and trembled whilst speaking.

"There's been a mob there all the morning," he added, excitedly, without waiting for an answer. "Every time I go to the door they shake their hats at me and shout. I can't learn what it is they want?"

"We have come to explain," said the Prefect, unable to help smiling at the Canon's startled appearance, "but we owe you an apology for not having come earlier. The secret is this, my dear M. Ponceau, we are using our influence to try and get you made a bishop, and the people somehow have got wind of our scheme."

"Me a bishop!" exclaimed M. Ponceau, standing

stockstill, with his two hands on his breast, and looking at us with perfect stupefaction.

We had not counted on his showing so much
surprise, and his emotion rather disconcerted us.

"You don't mean to say you would refuse a
bishopric?" says the Prefect amazed.

M. Ponceau passed his hand across his brow
and sat down without for the moment making any
reply. He seemed not yet able to realize what he
had heard, and took time to collect himself.

"Excuse me for this nervousness," he replied
at last, speaking in the soft voice habitual to him.
"The events of the morning have rather unsettled
me, and your communication is so unexpected that
I do not yet know what to say to it."

"We should all be so glad to see you a bishop!"
observes the Marquise gently.

"You have done me a great honour," answers M.
Ponceau, with quiet earnestness; "an honour such as
it needs a lifetime of gratitude to repay. But forgive me if I tell you that the honour is not one I
ever coveted. I know most men say this when they
are raised to dignities; but with me it is the truth.
I had grown to love the quiet life I lived here
amidst my books, and I have passed that age when
the prospect of entering upon a career of ambition
could compensate me for throwing off long-cherished

and familiar habits. What you offer me is a crown, Monsieur le Préfet, and crowns are always heavy when our heads have turned grey."

"Still, you must not refuse," pleads the Marquise.

"Nor do I, Madame," answers the priest. "I should be ashamed to decline an honour without having a better excuse than that it seemed to me irksome."

"That's well spoken, sir," says the General. "For my part, I don't think a man has any right to refuse honours; unless, that is, he feels too weak to bear them; which I am sure," adds the old soldier politely, "is not the case with you."

"We mustn't be going too far, however, and raising false hopes," interposes the Prefect, recalled to a sudden sense of realities by some more cheering outside. "Mind, we have not got you your bishopric yet, M. Ponceau; we are going to Paris about it to-day."

Here the Marquise and the Prefect's wife explained to the Canon how a petition had been drawn up for presentation to the Government, and how it was already covered with several thousand signatures. M. Ponceau listened and seemed touched. He had been quite sincere in asserting that he loved his present mode of life and was loth to leave it; but a man must be made of wood who can hear

unmoved that thousands of men are exerting themselves to do him honour, and are hailing his name
with shouts of goodwill. No doubt, had the amiable
Canon been able to peep behind the scenes and see
how the comedy of the petition had been started,
and what was the real intrinsic value of most of the
cheers he heard, he would have felt a considerable
number of illusions abandon him. But happily for
him, he could not see behind the scenes, and thus
had every reason to look proud and pleased at the
flattering recital that was made him. To have been
appointed bishop by the sole will of the Emperor or
one of his Ministers, would not have gratified him
over much; but to be raised to the episcopal chair
by the unanimous voice of his diocese was an honour
so great that, being really modest, M. Ponceau
could not help asking himself what he had done to
deserve it.

"Mind, we shall expect to hear some splendid
speeches from you at the Œcumenical Council;
where of course you will go to represent our diocese," smiles the Marquise.

"Depend upon it, Madame, that it will be my
constant effort to try and repay the kindness shown
me by representing Ville-Rosé worthily." And as
he spoke a flash of generous ambition gleamed before the Canon's eyes. He fancied he saw himself

standing amongst the bishops at St. Peter's and amazing them by his eloquence; and the thought of the pride which his diocese might feel at his triumphs, gave him the pleasure which gladdens an honourable man at the hope of repaying a benefactor.

But with all this it was getting time to be gone. The cathedral clock had chimed half-past three, and we had no more than an hour and a half before the train started. We accordingly took our leave of the Canon, who accompanied us to the door, no longer alarmed now by the tumult which burst out afresh as soon as we reappeared. He thanked us cordially for what we were doing for him, and shook hands with us all round.

"Good-bye, M. Ponceau," says the Prefect. "I hope this time to-morrow we may be back here with good news."

"You start at once?" asks the Canon from his doorway.

"Yes; at least we are going to call on the Abbé Bonneau first. We intend taking him with us to help plead your cause."

"Dear me! but I am afraid you will be disappointed of finding him," answers M. Ponceau. "I do not think he is here."

"Not here!" cries the Prefect, turning round.

"No. I called at his house yesterday, and they told me he had gone to Paris."

This was a strange piece of news that took us all aback. A journey to Paris on the part of the Abbé Bonneau was a thing so utterly unprecedented that, occurring at this particular juncture, it struck us as something ominous. The Abbé lived like an anchorite, never stirring beyond his parish. What could he possibly want in Paris, and at this moment too? We mused upon this question as we went along, and could find no feasible reply to it. The crowd, which had become perfectly convinced by this time that M. Ponceau had either been, or was just on the point of being, appointed bishop, followed us as closely as ever, and thought, no doubt, to give us pleasure by cheering and leaping, as if the Millennium had come. Some of the smaller citizens turned somersaults in the mud, to mark their keen appreciation of M. Ponceau's virtues; a few more struck up *Partant pour la Syrie*, to testify to their loyalty towards the Imperial dynasty. At the prefecture we stopped to take our carpet-bags and the famous petition, which had swelled in bulk to the size of a fine folio volume. In the excited state of public opinion we judged it scarcely prudent to have carriages to carry us to the station; for once a crowd has taken into its head to be enthusiastic, there is no knowing to what lengths it may go. It was just as likely as not that the mob, having nothing else to do, might, insist upon unharnessing our horses and dragging us in triumph round the market-place. We set out on foot, therefore, as previously, the ladies going with us to see us off, and five footmen marching behind with the luggage. On our way we called at the Abbé Bonneau's house, a small cottage with a thatched roof and a single chimney-pot. It had occurred to us that perhaps the Abbé had returned, or that at all events we might learn why he had gone. But we found him still away, and we could gather nothing from his housekeeper but that he had started off suddenly with his curate a few days ago upon receipt of a large letter in a blue envelope from Paris. This was too vague to help us much, but when we had turned away, the old woman, as if suddenly remembering an important clue, called out to us at the top of her voice that the letter had no stamp to it, but that there had yet been nothing to pay. This news caused the Prefect to arch his eyebrows, and the General to utter a formidable "Humph!" for the letters with no stamps on them and nothing to pay are usually the products of Government offices, and what the Abbé Bonneau could have to do with such, we were at a loss to understand.

Upon arriving at the station we found that we had still twenty minutes before us, and that a train was just coming in from Paris. We were all silent, pondering over the Abbé Bonneau's mysterious absence. The Marquise suggested he must have had a legacy. Madame la Générale wondered whether he had not been summoned to hear a lecture from the Minister of Justice upon his charitable prodigalities, which left him often with scarcely shoes to his feet. His Excellency the Minister was known to be a great stickler about the clergy maintaining a becoming appearance, and it was just possible he might have wished to inform M. Bonneau that a clergyman, with holes to his boots, is an object deserving of censure. We were in the midst of our speculations and doubts, when the Paris train came rumbling into the station, and whom should we see looking out of one of the windows, with his usually placid face, but this very Abbé Bonneau. It escaped none of us that he was travelling in a first-class carriage, and that his curate was sporting a new hat and a pair of black gloves, unaccustomed luxuries.

"Mon cher Monsieur Bonneau," says the Préfet, running forward and holding out his hand, "how delighted I am to see you!"

"This is really very good of you, Monsieur le

Préfet," falters the old man with beaming looks. "I didn't know the news had travelled so fast, but, to be sure, I had forgotten the telegraph. Thank you all kindly for coming to meet me; it's very thoughtful of you."

"Ahem!" coughs the Prefect, not quite understanding. "I suppose you have had a legacy, my dear Abbé. So Madame la Marquise thought, and we all beg to offer our congratulations. But, ahem! we are going to ask a favour of you, and we hope——"

"Anything in the world I can do to oblige you, Monsieur le Préfet," breaks in the poor old Abbé, perplexed.

"Well, it's just this," continues the Prefect, "and you will excuse us for being so abrupt, but the fact is, we have very little time before us. We have been getting up a petition in the diocese to have Canon Ponceau made Bishop of Ville-Rosé. We are going now to Paris to carry this petition to the Minister of Justice, and we want you to accompany us——"

"O mon Dieu!" stammers the old Abbé, becoming terribly red. "Then you have not heard the news yet."

"What news?" asks the Prefect, breathless.

"Why—why—O dear me, how sorry I am for all this, Monsieur le Préfet—why I have just come from

Paris—from the Minister of Justice—and the vacancy is filled up."

"Filled up!" cries the Prefect, aghast; "and by whom?" But he had no need to await a reply, for the Abbé's curate coming up at that moment, took off his hat, and said respectfully—

"The luggage is in the fly, *Monseigneur*."

Our new Bishop was the Abbé Bonneau.

L'AMBULANCE TRICOCHE.

L'AMBULANCE TRICOCHE:

RECOLLECTIONS OF THE SIEGE OF PARIS.

I.

MONSIEUR LE CURÉ TRICOCHE was a man of sense. He clothed himself warmly in winter; during the summer months he avoided exciting himself; and summer and winter he ate his dinner leisurely: "for if there is one thing I hate more than another," said he, "it is to be hurried whilst I am eating."

Nature had fitted him with a good round paunch, apt to contain any amount of *pâté-de-foie-gras;* and with a fine broad hand, made on purpose for the fingering of fees. He had a plump, honest face; wheezed a little when walking—the effect of the *foie-gras;* and if he had a two-sou piece in his pocket when a beggar passed, he gave him—his blessing.

Monsieur Tricoche had been helped up the ladder by a patron—so he liked patrons. His had been a M. de Roussis, a Voltairian, who supported the clergy, voted for the temporal power in the Corps Législatif, laughed at the Pope, and would not for the world

have undertaken a voyage on a Friday. M. de Roussis
was one of the "official deputies" of the Second Empire.   It is no disparagement to him to say that he
knew nothing: for had he known anything he would
not have been an official deputy; but he was a
pleasant, breezy, generous sort of a legislator, who
was fond enough of doing a good turn when it cost
him nothing; and so M. Tricoche, having at three
successive elections obtained for him the votes of
227 peasants, who could neither read nor write, he
had used his influence to have M. Tricoche appointed
to the incumbency of a spick-and-span new metro-
politan church, that of Ste. Rosemonde.

Everybody has seen and admired those spick-
and-span new Paris churches raised by the creative
genius of Baron Haussmann.   They are perfect.   Put
a check-taker at the door, and you might imagine
yourself entering a music-hall; ornament the façade
with a few yards of bunting, and there you have a
popular restaurant, a dry-goods' warehouse, a museum
of stuffed birds, or any other mortal thing you like
to fancy.   There is no doubt of this, that the archi-
tects of the Second Empire were true men, and
understood their business.   In these days of revolu-
tionizing, the main point to be avoided in building
is to give any edifice such a distinctive aspect as to
make its sudden transformation difficult.   It would

not be wise to make a church look like a church. To-morrow it might be converted into a "Temple of Reason," the next day into a club for advocating the Rights of Women. Moreover, so long as Herr von Bismarck lives, it is well to be prepared for the chance of its becoming a powder-magazine.

So the architect who constructed Ste. Rosemonde's had enriched it with a Gothic roof, a Byzantine dome, a Doric front, and a belfry that would have resembled a Chinese pagoda but for the Corinthian columns encircling it. The decorators, following in the wake, had painted the inside of the dome sky-blue, laid on an abundant coating of yellow-ochre over the walls, and spread gilding liberally, as if with a butter-knife, over every inch of cornice, beading, and pilaster. A distinguished artist had put the final touch. He had covered the yellow-ochre with cupids and dryads — some said they were cherubim and seraphim, but there was nothing to show it; traced his own signature in a garland between the interspaces of the arches; and devised for the altar a magnificent stained-glass window, which represented Adam and Eve being expelled from the garden of Eden, or the Genius of Napoleonism announcing the dawn of universal suffrage to two natives of the Fig-leaf Isles — it is not quite clear which. Authorities were agreed that the Church of Ste. Rosemonde was

3*

not such a church as you could meet with every day.
Baron Haussmann affirmed this, and so did the distinguished artist. And the members of the Opposition in the Chamber were of the same opinion, for
they said the church had cost four million francs.

But however this might be, Ste. Rosemonde's was
one of the most fashionable places of worship; and
when M. le Curé Tricoche arrived there, rustic and
hale, from a fifteen years' vicarage at Choufleury-
sur-Aube, he found himself pastor of as well-condi-
tioned a flock as any that a good priest could pray
for. All prosperous sheep they were, with abundance
of wool. Ste. Rosemonde's stood right in the centre
of a new quarter, built to lodge an interesting population of millionaires, who, having been without a
sixpence on the eve of the *coup-d'état*, and having
become rapidly rich posterior to that event, were
destitute of fitting places where to lay their heads.
Mansions in simili-marble, with gates in simili-bronze;
coach-houses at the back, gilt balconies to the front,
ready-made statues attitudinizing in the centre of
geranium-beds: all the dwellings in this neighbourhood were alike. You had no need to knock at the
door to be sure that the footmen wore brand-new
plushes and powder, that there were champagne
corks flying at luncheon, that Mdlle. Theresa's last
songs lay open on the piano, and that tickets for the

next ball at the Tuileries were to be seen on the mantel-shelf. All this was as visibly written over the stuccoed porticoes as if a scribe had done it. And you had not far to go to learn who the inmates were. Their names were in everybody's mouth and in the mundane gazettes. They were the birds of gay plumage who had built their nests in the branches of the Imperial trees.—The senators and deputies, ministers and stock-jobbers, field-marshals and opera-singers, Russian princes and Yankee tuft-hunters—all the men of the day, in short, who were making hay whilst the sun shone, persuaded that it would not last long, but that some morning or other, when they least expected it, the storm would come and scatter them to the four winds—them and the dynasty that had fattened them, their powdered footmen and their slippery millions, their mansions, sinecures, tinsel trappings, pinchbeck dignities, and that barley-sugar-looking church of theirs in which their wives and daughters praised Heaven every Sunday morning to *concerto* music at half-past eleven o'clock.

Now, you will not think, I hope, that I have undertaken this recital for the mere purpose of splashing ink at the Second Empire; or to tell you, as above, that M. le Curé Tricoche dearly loved his bit of turbot, his glass of "*Lafitte*, '46," and his fragrant cup of mocha after dinner. The Second

Empire — well, it is dead and buried now, so
requiescat; and as for M. Tricoche, why should I
grudge that worthy man his slice of fish and glass
of claret? For have I not seen him through the
perishing cold days of last winter striding, lean and
gaunt, beside the ambulance-waggons, and, after
twelve hours spent in shriving the dying and picking
up the wounded on the fields of Champigny and the
Plateau d'Avron, sit down to his ounce of under-
done horse-meat and his half-pound of gritty black
bread? "And quite good enough, too, for me, who
am the son of a peasant," would he say, with a quiet
smile; and turning to his old housekeeper, Mdlle.
Virginie, "Mind, my good Virginie, that what remains
in the cellar of that old Bordeaux is sent to the Ste.
Rosemonde ambulance to-morrow; and in future serve
me water."

I confess the change was a little startling. I remember visiting the Church of Ste. Rosemonde
about a year ago—no, it is not quite a year—it was
on that famous 8th May, 1870, when the Bonaparte
dynasty took a new lease of life, *auspice Æmilio*, M.
Emile Ollivier being chief of the cabinet. I fancy
M. Tricoche looked plumper than ever that morning.
He was in the pulpit. Below him twenty rows of
cushioned sittings were occupied by dresses from
Worth's, bonnets from Laure's, gloves from Jouvin's,

and chignons of any circumference you please to name. Down the lines gold-headed smelling-bottles glistened like batteries of field-pieces, and two hundred fans going *flap*, *flap* in unison kept up a concert that was infinitely refreshing, M. Tricoche was treating of a better world than this, where all there present would meet again. He did not say precisely what kind of a better world; but the impression conveyed was that one would find nothing but Bonapartists there, and that the good places would be reserved for official candidates. He denounced MM. Thiers and Jules Favre in pointed and vigorous (though anonymous) terms, formally excluding them from all share of paradise on the ground that by opposing that great and righteous National Measure, the Plebiscitum, they were proclaiming their unholy lust for bloodshed, their love of anarchy, etc., etc. Finally, he remarked that he would dismiss his hearers early that morning, for that some of them had a great civic duty to perform (*i. e.*, to go and vote "YES"); and so, "*Pax vobiscum, fratres, per sæcula sæculorum. Ite, missa est,*" and he waddled majestically into the sacristy.

The next time that I saw M. Tricoche was close upon four months after. Events had moved apace between the 8th May and the 4th September—that is, between the sowing of the seed and the garnering in of the harvest. Towards two p. m. on the latter of these two dates I found myself, together with something like a tenth of the population of Paris, in the vicinity of the Place de la Concorde. It was a sight to be never forgotten. The whole of that vast area was choked up with an excited, shouting sea of heads, swollen each minute with tributary torrents from the neighbouring streets, and surging in a compact mass towards the building of the Corps Législatif, where the Assembly were discussing the capitulation of Sedan. To the south, east, and west, in front of the Pont de la Concorde, the Tuileries, and the Champs Elysées, this tumultuous, seething lake was dyked in by lines of troops, whose glittering bayonets flashed in the sun of an absolutely cloudless sky—the sky of Austerlitz! The thickest dyke was along the quays, where the National Guards were arrayed, and the firmest on the Pont de la Concorde itself, where a troop of Cuirassiers were posted, grim, mounted, and looking game to die to the last man in case of need. Shall I acknowledge that I did not like the appearance of these Cuirassiers, and that, glancing at their long, drawn sabres, and then at the unprotected heads of the undulating multitude confronting them, I began to muse as to what it would be in a few minutes, when that multitude attempted to force the bridge and those sabres rose and fell, strewing gashed corpses around them by the dozen? As sure as I am now a living man, I expected bloodshed. I expected to see the death-signal start from the Quai d'Orsay, where I could discern a general's uniform, and, at the command, the whole columns of infantry open fire at once. We were a hundred and fifty thousand—ten thousand of us must have gone to our account, without remission, in the first five minutes. However, there was not a soul who blenched: on the contrary, the crowd grew denser, more determined; the revolutionary shouts rose louder and more fearless; the onward pressure gathered each second in intensity; and perhaps I was the only person in that countless assemblage who reflected that our lives now hung on a single thread, on the hazard of a chance collision between some drunken workman and quick-tempered soldier, or the momentary impulse for good or ill which might actuate that distant man in the uniform. "*A bas l'Empereur! La déchéance! A la Lanterne les Bonapartes!*" The soldiers closed up their ranks, and appeared to wait. "*Vive la Nation! A mort les Prussiens! Vive la France!*" I saw the soldiers hesitate. "*Vive l'Armée! Aux armes pour la patrie en danger! Vive l'heroïque ville de Strasbourg qui meurt pour rester avec nous!*" There was a thrill among the soldiers: they looked at one another, and then, in silence, reversed their arms. On the bridge the Cuirassiers sheathed their swords, and fell back. The Revolution was victorious without a blow. An immense cry, unanimous, resounding, and triumphant, rent the air: "*Vive la République, une, indivisible, et fraternelle!*" and with the force, freedom, and impetuosity of an inundation, the popular ocean swept headlong where it would.— to the Palace of the Assembly, to the Tuileries, to the Hôtel-de-Ville. As for me, I was caught up, whirled round in an eddy, and carried away like a wisp of straw, heaven knew whither. Workmen and soldiers arm-in-arm, become friends and brothers, were marching and singing; young girls laughed and cried, "*A bas l'Empire!*" small boys capered along and whistled. In front of the shops men on ladders were unhooking the Imperial scutcheons, throwing them down with a crash, and effacing the words, "*Purveyors to their Majesties,*" amid tremendous cheering. I should never have thought that deposing a dynasty could have been such gay work as that. Once or twice we had a stoppage at places where two roads met, and some travelling landau, with boxes on the roof, would pass by with the speed of the wind. It was not always easy to recognize the face inside; but occasionally a jolt would bring to view the ashen, scared features of an

ex-minister or senator *en route* for the railway-station;
and at this there would be terrific howling, not un-
mingled with derisive shouts of *"Bon voyage!"* and
valedictory stones. After all, it was a merry mob.
It bestowed an ovation upon a pork-butcher who had
hung up two defunct pigs in his window, crowned
them with gelatine, and labelled them respectively
"Bismarck" and "Napoleon;" and it halted frequently
before public-houses. Still, I should have been glad
enough to get clear of its company; and I was just
making my fourth or fifth effort to this end, attempting to elbow my way out of the current up a side-
street, when I found myself unexpectedly opposite
to the Church of Ste. Rosemonde.

As I have told you, I had not seen my friend
M. Tricoche for four months, but, fatality aiding, he
was on the steps at that minute, precisely as we
passed. I learned afterwards that he had been saying his mass and preaching his sermon before empty
seats, for the long-dreaded storm had come, and his
charming Worth-clad parishioners were most of them
flown to London. He seemed to me changed, careworn, and—strange to say—thinned. But he still
held himself straight, and sported on the breast of
his cassock the scarlet ribbon of the Legion of
Honour, with which he had been dignified the year
before, I forget for what reason. M. le Curé Tricoche

was too well-known a personage for the crowd to go
by him without an exchange of amenities. His presence at first occasioned mirth: everybody laughed
and stopped; and a burly workman, good-natured-
looking enough, despite the ferocious and com-
minatory attitude he struck, stepped out and apo-
strophized the good man:—

"Heigh there, M. le Curé, you know the Empire
has been despatched to kingdom-come, and you won't
refuse to join us in crying '*Vive la République!*' I
know?"

Must I own that I didn't think M. le Curé would
refuse. Indeed, why should he have done so, when
so many men greater than he were denying the idol
they had worshipped, and hastening to lay all dis-
asters, past, present, and future, to its charge. I
could not help smiling at what appeared to me the
naïveness of the workman in supposing the prosperous, acute M. Tricoche would risk a broken head
for the sake of defending such a sorry, friendless
thing as a fallen Power. What was not then my
surprise, my confusion, when, fixing a mild glance
on the man, the Curé said:—

"My good friend, when the Emperor declared
war, not six weeks ago, I was among the men who
approved him, encouraged him, and I have been
humiliating myself ever since for that bad action

The Emperor is paying much less for faults of his own than for sins of ours, who, able to prevent his unwise enterprises, never had the honesty to do so. I do not know what has been the part you have played in this war, nor what it would have been had our armies proved victorious; but for myself let me say that if the Emperor had come back in triumph, I should have cheered him; you will excuse me, therefore, if in this hour of his defeat I cry, '*Vive l'Empereur!*' all the same, and add this other cry, 'God save France, and forgive me for my share in her present calamities.'"

This was said simply, without faltering, but without ostentation. The blush of shame rose to my face, and furtively I crept beside M. Tricoche, ready to stand between him and any awkward consequences his courageous words might entail. But mobs are sometimes not ungenerous. The workman stared a moment, then shrugged his shoulders and turned away, rather bewildered, I fancy, and wondering within himself what curious breed of a man this could be who felt he had done wrong and quietly said so. The rest of the crowd trudged on at the heels of the workman, wondering also why the Curé had not shouted as he was bid, but yelling "*Vive la République!*" with all their own mights to make up for the loss. As for me, left alone with the Curé, I saluted him with respect. It seemed to me that in these few minutes he had grown a cubit.

II.

The excellent man's conversion, as it was good-naturedly called, created some sensation — not so much at the time itself, however, as a few weeks afterwards. During the fortnight that elapsed between the proclamation of the Republic one and indivisible, and the investment of Paris, people were too much occupied with their own business to concern themselves about other people's. The Republicans were distributing posts of emolument to one another; such of the Bonapartists as had not already decamped were hastening to do so; moreover, it was the time for the general laying in of provisions. Every morning long lines of carts entered Paris loaded with cheeses and the new Provisional Government, with an eye to the future, caused these cheeses to be transported to underground cellars, where they got nice and mouldy. Everybody invested more or less in sardines, sacks of unchewable sea biscuit, tins of concentrated soup, labelled with incomprehensible directions, and jars of potted meat exported from England by intelligent speculators, who, deeming the occasion a fine one, had hit upon the plan of filling a good number of the jars with tallow, and leaving us to find out the joke a few months later, when we had nothing else to eat. There were also fire-proof and shell-proof precautions to be taken with the roofs of our dwelling-houses, by means of layers of earth, which the winter snows, by the way, frequently converted into salubrious reservoirs of liquid mud;—and all these pre-occupations debarred the public from paying much attention to M. Tricoche. But by-and-by when the siege was fairly commenced; when the booming of the cannon had already become familiar music to our ears; when, in short, the Parisians found leisure to count themselves, and see who were the faithful who had remained to share the ordeal, who the patriots who "would have so liked to stay," but had been ordered away just at this unfortunate moment to Brighton or Nice by their doctors—then, it began to be noticed in the parish of Ste. Rosemonde that M. le Curé Tricoche was no longer the man he was be-fore, that he had given up wheezing, that his head was greyer, and that somehow or other people no longer felt tempted to laugh when he passed them as in the good old days when his rubicund visage and waddling gait struck all beholders with mirth.

Nevertheless, it was not good to accept this transformation without suspicion. One must be wary now-a-days. After all, M. Tricoche was a rich man.

He had been pocketing the revenues of Ste. Rosemonde (estimated at 100,000 francs per annum) for
now several years; he had two horses in his stable;
his cassocks were lined with satin; it was notorious
that roast-meats figured at his board. This new
sanctimonious attitude of his might only be some
Jesuitic feint destined to throw dust into the eyes
of the Republic one and indivisible. Who knows?

Mind you, these are not my views, but they
were those of one or two good citizens who were
disinterested enough to meddle with matters that
did not concern them, for the purpose, as they expressed it, of finding out what was what. These
citizens laid their heads together; they whispered.
Like a drop of oil on a flooring, the notion began
to spread that it behoved the cautious to look
closely after the Curé Tricoche; and one evening
the Vicar of Ste. Rosemonde—"that fox in sheep's
clothing, that disciple of Loyola, whose ways were
dark and tiger-like,"—was made the subject of a
solemn and formal denunciation at the "Club Dé-
mocratique et Social des Fils de Brutus," the Citizen
Christophe Bilia in the tribune.

He was a great man, this Citizen Bilia, and a
fervid patriot, who howled and raved and made the
rafters shake whenever he talked about tyranny.
No one knew much respecting his antecedents.

Some said they had met him in ministerial ante-
chambers, begging favours under the Second Empire.
But this was evidently a lie — a scurrilous insult
against the Sovereign People—a venomous calumny
which the Citizen Bilia cast back into the teeth of
his traducers with the utmost loathing and contempt.
The only thing known for certain about M. Bilia
was that on the 4th of September, seeing posts of
dignity and profit scattered about broadcast, but
himself forgotten in the distribution, he had arrived
at the conclusion that the word Republic would
cease to have any sense if it did not mean that
every citizen was at liberty to choose the post that
suited him best, and to fix his own salary out of
the public purse. In consequence, he had gone
quietly and installed himself in a Government office
—pay, 20,000 francs—hung his hat on a peg, called
for refreshments, and, in a word, comported himself
so much as if he had been in place all his life, that
the new chief of the department supposed he had
got an appointment duly signed and sealed in his
pocket, and only discovered his mistake something
like a fortnight afterwards. Perhaps even then M.
Bilia might have succeeded in retaining his post
had his work been sufficient and his accounts correct—for at best it is rather a delicate business for
a Republican who has helped himself to a bunch of

seals to turn out another Republican who has only helped himself to a First-Secretaryship. But unfortunately M. Bilia objected to work, and his accounts were not correct. He was expostulated with. He yelled. It was pointed out to him civilly that two and four made six and not three in most addition sums. He proclaimed his conviction that the Government was rotten, vowed that he would be no party to reactionary machinations, and indignantly threw down his resignation — an act of magnanimity which, however, cost him nothing: for the National Guard elections happening to be then afoot, a battalion of brother patriots hastened to mark their sense of the indignity the Citizen M. Bilia had suffered by electing him to be their chief. In this capacity he was qualified to wear embroidered clothing, to drag a steel scabbard with a sword inside it wherever he went, and even to fight the Prussians if ever he found leisure and inclination for that purpose—which, be it remarked, he seldom did, being probably otherwise engaged. Such was the gentleman who scaled the tribune on public grounds to tell "The Sons of Brutus" what his opinion was concerning M. Tricoche.

The meeting was stormy that night—in fact, it was every night stormy. "The Sons of Brutus" was one of those numerous and enjoyable clubs where, the theatres being closed, the besieged population resorted to divert itself a little of an evening. The subjects for debate were varied. If a Son of Brutus was dunned by his shoemaker he came here and held up that black-hearted oppressor to contumely. If two Republicans fell out and kicked one another, it was odds but they both came here in the course of the sitting and exchanged flavoured epithets tending to show that each was in the pay of Count von Bismarck. Political questions were also discussed: the Government was declared felon, idiot, and corrupt, thirty or thirty-one nights a month, as the case might be, and the evening was generally terminated by the hooting down and unceremonious bundling out of some orator who had expressed sentiments at variance with those of the majority. This was the usual programme; but what "The Sons of Brutus" loved above all things was to give up a sitting exclusively to the compilation of a list of "traitors" (selected from the public men of the day—ministers, generals, liberal journalists, etc.), with a view to dealing summarily with them on the day when they, "The Sons of Brutus," got into office. It was naturally one of these "traitor" nights that M. Bilia selected for the remarks he wished to utter about the Curé of Ste. Rosemonde.

Seven o'clock had struck. The concert-room in

4*

which "The Sons of Brutus" held their sittings was crammed tight-full as usual, the predominant element being blousy—that is, clad in blouses—though there were women present, and here and there— *rari nantes in gurgite vasto*—a black coat or two, objects of suspicion and mistrustful glances. Custom demanded that the meeting should every evening elect its board, the chair being occupied during that formality by the president chosen the night before. A board consists of an honorary president (often defunct but illustrious), an effective president, two assessors, and a secretary. The preceding night the Citizen Joshua, "slayer of five and thirty kings," had been elected to the honorary chairmanship amidst uproarious cheering. This evening an emaciated citizen, with long finger-nails, rose from one of the back benches and, in a shrill treble, moved—"That the Greek citizen Aristogiton be voted into the chair."

A Citizen with a red beard, springing up furiously.—"Citizens, I protest. How does that man dare to move that a Greek aristocrat named Giton shall be voted into the chair at a meeting of Republicans? Down with all *aristos*, say I." (Vehement applause. Looks of indignation at the emaciated citizen. Cries of "Turn him out.")

The Citizen Maclou (in the chair).—"Citizen, I

call upon you to explain what you mean by insulting this Republican assembly."

The Emaciated Citizen.—"Citizen President, there is a mistake. The man who interrupted me is an idiot. Aristogiton is the name of a Greek *sans-culotte*, who slew the last of the Pisistratids, a race of despots and vampires like the Bonapartes. Aristogiton restored the Republic." (Murmurs of incredulity; faint applause.)

A Citizen with a basket to a Citizen with a bottle. — "That chap knows too much! I shouldn't be surprised if he were a *mouchard.*"

The Citizen with the bottle to the Citizen with the basket.—"I don't like the look of him. And why does he come talking to us about a Greek President —as if Frenchmen weren't good enough for the post?"

The Citizen with the red beard.—"That man calls me an idiot! I expect he's some thief, if not worse. Anyhow, he's a liar! He says the Aristo Giton restored the Republic. I don't believe it. I say that an aristo never restored anything to anybody— never." (Great cheering. Cries to the emaciated citizen, who vociferates something: "Hold your row." "Put your head in a bag.") "Citizens, I am not afraid of that man; if he comes here to the front I'll thrash him in two minutes. Don't have anything

to do with his candidate. Here's another that'll
do better: he's a Latin citizen whose name I read
in the paper, the Citizen Germanicus, who licked
the Germans, and was a thorough-going radical."
(Acclamations. Prolonged applause. The Citizen
Germanicus is elected honorary president. The
emaciated citizen, continuing to vociferate, is seized
by the legs and arms and ejected with ignominy.)

The election of the Acting Board then ensues.
The Citizen Maclou, who has hinted that he has no
intention of moving, is confirmed in his place, and
his assessors with him. A citizen who has im-
prudently confided to somebody that he is a writing-
master, is forced into the secretary's seat. He objects that he must go at ten, being on duty that
night as a National Guardsman on the ramparts;
but the remonstrance only has the effect of bringing
a couple of citizens to keep an eye on him, to the
right and left, and prevent his bolting.

The President Maclou.—"Citizens, we shall proceed this evening with our list of traitors, but
before that let any citizen who has general observations to make, get up and make them."

A Citizen with a squint stands up and declares
that he withholds his esteem from the Citizen Jules
Favre, Minister of Foreign Affairs. (Hear, hear.)
Not that he ever expected much from a citizen

who has interviews with Bismarck (groans) and signs himself in writing the "obedient servant" of that ruffian (renewed groans), but he had never gauged the full measure of the Citizen Favre's unworthiness until that morning. Having a communication of importance to make to the Government, he had called at Favre's residence, and been kept waiting an hour in an ante-room, at the end of which time a menial with a white cravat round his throat, badge of slavery, had come and informed him that if he wished to see the Minister he must apply in writing for an audience. It was evident that the Citizen Favre was endeavouring to ré-implant in a free land the degrading formalities existing in countries governed by tyrants. He moved that the Citizen Favre be set up in the pillory of public opinion, be pronounced traitor and outlaw, and that all true patriots be enjoined to refuse him obedience. (General marks of assent. Applause.)

A Citizen slightly drunk thinks poorly of the Citizen Ernest Picard, Minister of Finances. He too—the citizen slightly drunk—had a communication of importance to make to the Government. He had invented a new shell, which was one of the most murderous ever fabricated, and would very soon get rid of the Prussians. Here it was, he had a model of it in his pocket. If he dropped this shell on the floor everybody in the room would be blown away to atoms. (Sensation.) Ay, and it would be precious difficult to find the bits, he could tell them that. (Renewed sensation.) Well, he had applied to the Citizen Picard for a subsidy to help him push his invention, and Picard had declined to lend him a centime. What business had the Citizen Picard to give himself these airs. Did he think the purse of the nation was his? Who filled those money-bags which he guarded like the dog in the manger? It was not the Citizen Picard himself, I fancy. (Hear, hear.) No, it was the people, with the sweat of their brows; and this conduct of the Minister of Finance was but part and parcel of the old system followed by all governments, of keeping the working man out of what justly belonged to him. He moved that the Citizen Picard be summoned to tender his resignation without delay. (Hear, hear. Applause. The citizen retires with his shell to a front bench, which is expeditiously vacated by its occupants, who install themselves at a prudent distance.)

Three Citizens rise together and inveigh—the first, at a grocer of the Rue St. Denis, who has refused to let him take away sixteen pounds of bacon on credit, as if his word wasn't as good as those of the aristocrats whom the same grocer trusted to any extent they pleased. (Hear, hear.) The second, at his landlord, who has given him notice to quit when the siege is over, on the pretext that though he, the citizen, is earning four francs a day, he has declined to pay his rent ever since the beginning of the war, and stated his intention of not disbursing the arrears even when the peace is signed.* (Great cheering.) And the third, at the Citizen Arago, Mayor of Paris, who, having been repeatedly memorialized to change the names of streets which recall the brutalizing superstitions of past ages — notably the names of saints and priests—has signified his peremptory refusal. He, the third citizen, lives in the Rue St. Onge, and feels degraded at having to give such an address to his friends. He does not see why his self-respect should be obliterated to please the Citizen Arago. (Cheers and expressions of sympathy.)

A Citizen in a black coat.—"Perhaps I can appease the citizen's susceptibilities. The name of the street is not *Saint Onge*, but *Saintonge*—one word only. Saintonge is the name of an old French province." (Interruption. Murmurs. Cries of "Order!")

The Third Citizen.—"If the citizen in the black coat has come here with the intention of humiliat-

---

* It will be remembered that persons paying less than 600 francs rent were absolved by Government decrees from all obligations towards their landlords so long as the war lasted.

ing the people, I may tell him that he and his manœuvres excite only disgust and contempt." (Loud cheers. Cries of "Turn him out!")

The Citizen with the basket to the Citizen with the bottle.—"He looks like a Jesuit in disguise."

The Citizen with the bottle to the Citizen with the basket.—"Yes, I know those Jesuits. My wife used to go and confess herself to one of them, and——" (He proceeds with developments.)

The President Maclou.—"I close the incident. These interruptions are offensive. I beg to tell the Citizen in the black coat, and all like him, that this is a club of equality, and that those who have the pretension of knowing more than their neighbours had better remain outside." (Cordial and unanimous applause.) "And now to business. We shall proceed with our roll of those who, by reason of their conduct, public or private, deserve to be placed on the people's list of felons and traitors, there to be pointed at with the finger of scorn and universally execrated, until the day of expiation shall arrive, and the Democratical, Social, Communistical Republic shall have justice meted out to them. There are several orators inscribed. I call upon the Citizen Faggeaux to make himself heard."

Cries from all parts of the hall.—"Citizen Faggeaux to the tribune!"

A Female Citizen with vigorous lungs.—"Faggeaux has sent me here to say he can't come. Those dogs of policemen are looking after him because he knocked down a colonel of infantry who insulted him this morning. I'm Faggeaux's maid; that's why he sent me." (Cheers. Expressions of sympathy for the Citizen Faggeaux.)

The President Maclou.—"This meeting, by the mouth of its president, conveys its regrets and condolence to the Citizen Faggeaux, who has courageously buffeted prætorianism. The next name on the list is that of the Citizen Crappolle."

A Citizen with a black eye.—"I'm Crappolle's brother. Crappolle is in the Mobile, and just because, being on guard at the outposts yesterday, he ran back into Paris to fetch his pocket-handkerchief, which he had forgotten, his captain has punished him with a fortnight's *salle de police*, and even threatened to have him up before a court-martial." (Murmurs of indignation.) "Ah! I know what it is. Those aristocrats would like to get Crappolle killed because he's a Republican. This is the second time they've sent him to the outposts, but he knows their game as well as I do, and he's not going to let himself be killed to amuse them." (Loud cheers. Cries of "Quite right!")

The President Maclou.—"Such being the case, I

call upon the Citizen Christophe Bilia, who comes third on the list, to stand up and speak." (Applause. Attention.)

The Citizen Bilia, in the uniform of *chef-de-bataillon*, and girded with an imposing scarlet sash. —"Citizens, I am a plain man, and whenever I've got anything to say, I say it. There are, no doubt, some *mouchards* in this assembly, for the occult agents of despotism are a vermin who swarm everywhere; but I don't care for them, not I, and I'm glad that they should be present, in order to learn that if the Republic one and indivisible sends forth its sons to combat the foreign foe, it also takes care to keep its eye upon those more dangerous vipers who lurk in its own bosom—those sinister hirelings of dethroned tyrants who are allowed to herd together and conspire within our very walls—those white-livered renegades who, under the name of Republicans, govern our affairs, and plot secretly to betray us into the hands of Bismarck; and, worse than all, those hypocrite myrmidons of the Pope of Rome, who, whilst pretending to give us their prayers, fatten upon our alms, and in their heart of hearts pray for the day when the crowned savage of Germany shall enter our city with his barbarian hordes, crush our new-born Republic under his horse's hoofs, and bring us back in his train some king or emperor, even as the Demon of Death, when he scours the plain, brings a troop of carrion vultures after him." (Thundering applause. Excitement.) "Citizens, it gives me pleasure to see that our list of traitors is swelling. There are at present two thousand three hundred and ninety-seven names upon it, the last being that of the Citizen Trochu; for whom, as you rightly declared in your vote of last Tuesday, the vocabulary of known languages contains no epithets sufficiently stigmatizing. To-day I propose to add another name to the roll; it will form a fitting pendant to that of Trochu—for what tallies better with a Puritan despot than a canting bigot? what matches more suitably with a psalm-singing, freedom-oppressing, Prussian-fearing general, than a smooth-visaged, tortuous-minded priest, who bears candour on his face and turpitude in his soul, words of patriotism on his lips, and thoughts of treachery, rapine, and villainy in his ignoble heart? Citizens, I denounce to public indignation the Abbé Tricoche, Curé of Rosemonde." (Three rounds of applause.) "You all of you know that flaunting church, that gilded charnel-house, where the tainted creatures of the Second Empire paraded their ribbons and jewels, as the lepers of the East exposed their sores in the porches of the temples. Why was it not swept away with the Empire that produced it? Why was it not razed to the ground, and a gibbet-board set up in its place, saying, '*This is the spot where Religion made herself the handmaid of Cæsarism, fawned to it, licked the mire off its feet, and threw the cloak of priestly absolution over its crimes?*'" (Great cheering. Growing excitement.) "Citizens, I passed by that church this morning; I entered it, and what did I see? The place had been transformed into a hospital for the wounded; there were beds in it, stoves to warm it, a display of bandages and medicine-bottles—all the apparel, in short, of decent charity. But when I turned to see whose were the hands that administered these things, judge of the feelings that welled up within me when I perceived a part of that brazen crew who but a few months since used this same church for their vanity-airing ground. Going from bed to bed, with eyes turned heavenwards, the Citizen Tricoche; in a corner, mixing a potion, the Countess of something or other, who not a year ago set all the scandal-papers mad with her eccentric disguises at the Court masked balls, and who now, to keep up her masquerading traditions, had travestied herself as a Sister of Mercy; and in the midst of this scene, strutting about with astonishing effrontery in a private soldier's uniform, a pomaded coxcomb with a glass in his eye, an ex-dandy of the Bois de Boulogne

—a son of a Bonapartist outlaw, the Minister Robache!" (Considerable sensation. Explosion of murmurs. Cries of "To the *lanterne* with them.") "Citizens, it is time that the comedy should cease. Since when do ghouls gloat thus openly over their work in the broad light of day? Are we children that we should be deluded by these pitiful farces? Shall the sanctimonious grimaces of a priest, the stagey ministrations of a patchouli-scented countess, the affected uniform of an impudent fop, make us forget that it is these people—this priest, countess, and fop—who have helped to let loose the hell-hounds of War on us, and that were they to pass twelve hours of their day in bathing wounds, and the other twelve in rolling their heads in the dust, they could not stanch a hundred thousandth part of the blood they had caused to flow, nor dry a single one of the tears that have been shed through their wanton doings?" (An ominous thrill through the hall. The eyes of certain citizens begin to gleam. Fists are clenched.) "Heigh, citizens, we are not women, I think. These people are braving us. Are you the men to stand that court lacqueys shall thus flourish their buffoon antics in the face of your grief; or can I rely upon a hundred resolute patriots to accompany me to-morrow, and call these menials out of livery to their senses? We will tell that

countess to begone where she pleases — to some
land where the carnival still continues, to Rome, or
to Monaco, or, if she likes it better, to London,
where the rest of the clique are; the balloons will
take her. Young Robache, he shall go to the outposts: perhaps some bullet will do him the honour
to touch him, though steel and lead which make
war on soldiers, mostly disdain to harm curs of his
breed. As for the hoary old priest, his presence is
a scandal; let him be turned out of the church his
abject servility has polluted. Let him run away;
there are garrets enough where he can hide his
shame until the siege is over; and if he refuses to
go—why, let the consequences be on his own head:
he will not be the first priest whom patriots have
had the courage to put out of the way when the interests of public morality and decency demanded
it. Tell me, are there a hundred fearless men
among you I can rely on?" (Immense howling.
Three or four hundred dusky fists are brandished
aloft, whilst yells of "To the gibbet the priests," "To
the scaffold the aristocrats," make the club-room ring
again.)

A Citizen dressed as a National Guardsman,
springing up suddenly, pale but determined.—
"Citizens . . . Citizens—one word. I am unknown
to most of you, but I am a working-man like your-

selves, and in the name of that freedom which you claim as a right, I stand up to protest—to protest with all my might against the speech you have just heard." (Exclamations. Stupefaction.) "Yes, let me speak. So long as the Citizen Bilia confined himself to mere word-attacks on the Government I kept silent, although, let me say, that for one who is himself an officer, to revile his military superior as the Commandant Bilia did General Trochu, seems to me an example of indiscipline one cannot too strongly deplore. But I should have paid less attention to that had it not been for the latter part of the Citizen Bilia's speech. Citizens, I adjure you, let us have no factions in the presence of the enemy. We all at this moment stand with one foot in the grave. Listen." (Deep silence. The faint boom of a cannon resounds in the distance.) "By that sound, citizens, which may be the death-knell of brothers of ours, I entreat you, I implore you, let us remain united. There can be no hostility between Bonapartist and Republican to-day, when both to-morrow may be lying side by side under the same sod. There cannot—there must not be hatred between hearts in which throbs one common love of our afflicted country—one common hope for her triumph, her regeneration. Let us forget the past—it is behind us; let us link our hands, our arms, our

strength, our prayers, and look to the future. If there
be hypocrites or traitors in our midst, Heaven help
them! but do not let us accept the thought, for the
shame of treachery in such hours as these recoils,
not on one head alone, but on a whole community.
Rather let us give every man credit for such patriotism as he may claim, and if we see around us women, priests, and young men, whom we have known
frivolous in days gone by, let us gladly and proudly
note any change we may observe in them, taking it
as an earnest that our poor France is not the demora-
lized nation which her enemies pretend, but that her
children can still, in the hour of need, cast aside
their foibles and devote their best, purest energies
to her service.   Citizens, it is not a Bonapartist, an
Orleanist, or a Legitimist, who is now addressing
you, but a Republican.   And not a Republican of
yesterday, but one who has lived all his life in the
same faith, who has constantly held by the device,
'Liberty, Equality, Fraternity,' but who has thought,
and still thinks, that the noblest of these three words
is Fraternity."   (Conflicting manifestations.   A few
cheers.   Predominant cries of "No, no.   Sit down."
"No milk-and-water Republican!")

The Citizen Bilia.—"Citizens, I denounce that
man as a traitor and an enemy to his country.   His
sentiments might pass muster in a nun's conventicle,

but uttered before an assembly of free men, who are not to be duped by child's play—they are a mockery and an insult." (Loud cheers.) "There can be no forgiveness for the men of the past; between us and them it is a war to the knife." (Renewed and prolonged cheering.) "The citizen throws the word fraternity in our teeth, well knowing that under present circumstances the mere mention of such a name is a division. Fraternity! where was it on the night of the 2nd December, '51? Did those men think of fraternity when they pressed the working-man's throat under their foot, and poured out his blood into the gutter? Fraternity! were they softened by the word when they saw our brothers rotting in the pontoons of Cayenne, and dying like dogs in the casemates of Lambessa? Citizens, there can be no fraternity between men and wolves. The fraternity shall be between us who have old scores to pay off, and if we ever consent to draw a sponge over the past, it will only be on that day when our debt shall have been discharged drop for drop, and tooth for tooth—when we shall have made the rich disgorge the wealth they have plundered—when we shall have wrested from them the liberties they have robbed and the privileges they have confiscated. Citizens, it will be time enough to talk of fraternity when equality exists, and there are no more task-

5*

masters; when we shall no longer see men feasting
in gilded palaces whilst their brothers die of hunger
in garrets." (Cheers, howls, gnashing of teeth, and
shaking of fists. Enthusiastic ovation to the Citizen
Bilia. The *National Guardsman* utters some words
inaudible in the tumult. *A Citizen*, with a clay pipe,
smites him on the cheek, whereupon a scuffle ensues, in which the gentleman who struck the first
blow does not get the best of it. Some other
citizens, partisans of equality, at once intervene, and
place matters on a fairer footing by setting upon the
National Guardsman ten or twelve to one. They
pinion him, roll him over, pull his coat to pieces,
and bundle him out into the street. Great cheering.)

The Citizen Maclou.—"Nobody can pretend that
the fullest liberty of discussion is not allowed here;
but when persons come with the evident intention
of railing at the sufferings of the people, they must
be prepared for the consequences." (Unanimous
assent.)

The sitting soon after breaks up. The Citizen
Bilia rises to go, and is followed by nine-tenths of
the audience, who accompany him with flattering
demonstrations, patting him on the back and cheering him lustily. It is arranged that there shall be
a rendezvous of "The Sons of Brutus" on the mor-

row to pay a visit to the Citizen Tricoche, and have
an hour's quiet talk with him. The time of the
meet is, however, kept a secret—it is always well to
be cautious. At the door, going out:—

*The Citizen with the basket to the Citizen with the
bottle.*—"That man in the National Guard's uniform
was undoubtedly an agent of Bismarck's."

*The Citizen with the bottle to the Citizen with the
basket.*—"I am sure of it. That Prussian has spies
everywhere. I never go to sleep without first looking under my bed, and yesterday I saw a pair of
boots peeping out. The boots were mine, you know,
but you can understand what a start it gave me at
first. I assure you, if I hadn't had this bottle. . . ."
(Exeunt fraternally, making one another's flesh
creep.)

III.

I happened to be present at this meeting of
"The Sons of Brutus" which I have just described.
I attended there in a journalistic capacity; but, as
our craft is not adored by the gentlemen of the
popular clubs, I generally concealed my identity
under a National Guard *képi*, ensconced myself in
the most retired nook of the gallery, and, during the
prevalence of hostilities between rival factions, main-

tained that dignified non-intervention attitude which
Great Britain has set in fashion. Walking home,
however, through the moonlit streets, it occurred to
me that I should perhaps do well to reflect on what
step it behoved me to take now in the face of the
avowed intention of "The Sons of Brutus" to make
an armed incursion on the domain of M. Tricoche.
To be sure, had I wished to model my conduct
strictly on that of Great Britain aforesaid, I need not
have meditated long. All I had to do was to take
a sheet of paper, and write a feeling despatch to
the Citizen Bilia, reminding him that this was the
nineteenth century, that we were in a civilized age,
that it was, perhaps, a pity to molest one's neighbour; but that, anyhow, if he thought otherwise, and
persisted in assaulting the Curé Tricoche, plunder-
ing his church, and finally hanging him to a lamp-
post, he might count upon my strictest neutrality.
This done, I should have folded my arms, and taken
heaven to witness that, if bloodshed ensued, it was
no fault of mine. By-and-by, when M. Tricoche
was hanged, the church gutted, and the Citizen Bilia
loaded with spoil, I might have reappeared on the
scene in the character of mediator, made some more
allusions to the nineteenth century, paid some new
compliments to modern civilization, and proposed to
-M. Bilia to surrender part of his lootings. On his

refusal, I should have begged him to believe that my esteem for him remained unaltered, and expressed the hope that the amicable relations subsisting between us would continue serene till the end of time.

Somehow, I could not help thinking that, however elevated and spirited this kind of policy might be in the case of nations, it had its inconveniences as between man and man. And the main inconvenience was, that it would not have saved M. Tricoche. So I preferred doing what, in diplomatic language, is called "casting about for alliances." In other words, I went to the police-station.

"Ah!" said the "Guardian of the Peace" to whom I unfolded my tale, "I see what it is: they're going to be at their old tricks again. That Bilia is a bad 'un!"

He was a smug policeman, shaved all but his whiskers, and his manners were calm, serious, and pensive. He was one of that new brigade of police formed by the Prefect, M. de Kératry, who had laid a ruthless hand on the sergents-de-ville of the Second Empire, suppressing their moustaches, their cocked hats, and even their title.

"Yes," I answered, glad to find him so impressionable, "I am inclined to agree with you about the Citizen Bilia."

"Humph!" he proceeded, shaking his head. "I know their games. They get all together, under pretence of politics and such like, and when they've speechified a bit, they break the windows and they rob. It's always the same story."

"Then, I conclude, you see the necessity of taking prompt measures to repress this attempt."

"Yes," said he. "I'll just send one of my men round to this Bilia, and talk to him a bit. If that won't do, I'll ask you to be good enough to let me know if anything happens to-morrow—if they do any mischief, I mean—then, I'll see if we can't manage to catch a few of them; but not this Bilia —he'd give us too much trouble."

Evidently this worthy man had mistaken his vocation. Nature had intended him for an English foreign minister. I departed, heaving something like a sigh of regret over those not very distant times when half-a-dozen words to the police would have been enough to ensure the Citizen Bilia's being arrested in his bed, conveyed under escort to Mazas, and lodged there at Government expense until he had had time to cool. It is true that now we were in the enjoyment of Republican institutions, which means that it was no longer lawful to arrest a criminal until he had actually committed that which he was bent upon, and not quite prudent to do it even then if he were, like the Citizen Bilia, a man holding repute among the people. You see, there are shades of opinion in these things, which it is well to comprehend. To plunder in the name of hunger, want, and cold is undoubtedly a crime; but to do the same thing in the name of liberty, equality, and fraternity is mistaken zeal—nothing more.

So, having failed in my first negotiation for allies, I addressed myself elsewhere. I sought out an acquaintance, a colonel of Breton Mobiles, whose sympathy for Republicans was small, and who had never, that I am aware, heard talk of non-intervention. This time my errand was not bootless. The colonel stroked his moustache significantly, despatched an estafette to the War Office to ask for powers, and in less than two hours, having *carte blanche* in his pocket, gave his orders for a march out at daybreak. The next morning, on arriving before the church of Ste. Rosemonde, I found my friend quietly picketed in the vicinity with his eight hundred men, and waiting for events. •

I should have had some difficulty in knowing Ste. Rosemonde's again but for these Mobiles. At the first rumour of a probable siege and bombardment, the distinguished architect of the building, seized with terror at the thought of his master-work being chipped, and possibly, too, struck with some

misgiving as to the resisting power of the edifice in
case it should have any but very undersized shells
to encounter, 'had applied to the Government for I
forget how many hundred sacks of earth, a request
which had been graciously acceded to. These sacks
had been used to pad the walls and roof, and the
church looked as though it were being treated for
influenza. On the belfry, besacked out of all shape,
a white flag, with the now familiar red cross, fluttered
lazily in the breeze; and on the church door, sur-
mounted also with a red cross, one could read this
announcement: "*Ambulance of Ste. Rosemonde.* 150
*beds. By permission of Monseigneur the Archbishop
of Paris, this church will be used during the siege as
a military ambulance. Divine service will be celebrated
every day in the Sacristy, temporarily converted into
a chapel.*"

Thus the Citizen Bilia had not erred, and the
once fashionable Ste. Rosemonde's had truly become
a hospital. There was a pasted notice inside the
vestibule praying visitors to walk softly and to speak
low; the alms-box formerly labelled, "*Pour les
Pauvres,*" bore the inscription: "*Pour les Blessés.*"
When one pushed the inner folding-doors, it was no
longer to step into an atmosphere of music, incense,
and radiant vestments; but the same sad, quiet scene
met the gaze as is to be witnessed wherever the sick

are congregated—long, tranquil rows of white beds
lit up in this instance by the few rays struggling
faintly through the half-barricaded windows and by
two papers burning perpetually over the altar. Two
lateral chapels, which in days gone by had blazed
with light, flowers, and votive offerings, had been
appropriated, the one to a pharmacy, the other to a
linen-room; and instead of the gilded *Suisse* and
silver-stick vergers, one or two Sisters of Mercy
glided about noiselessly between the beds, carrying
soothing potions, lint, and bandages under the direction of a grey man in list slippers (the military
surgeon). A life-size figure of the Saviour on the
Cross, mournfully yet fitly completed this picture of
human suffering and seemed to sanctify it.

Yes, the Citizen Bilia had spoken correctly; yet
there was one thing he had forgotten to add,
probably deeming it immaterial, and that was the
names of the persons who had founded and were
now supporting the ambulance of Ste. Rosamonde
at a cost of something like six thousand francs a
week. They were not many, only three, but, oddly
enough, they were the very M. Tricoche, whom M.
Bilia proposed to turn out; Mdme. la Comtesse de
Verveine, whom he thought of despatching to Monaco
per balloon to join in the carnival; and M. Robache,
the young gentleman who wore an eyeglass, and

also, M. Bilia might have mentioned, his arm in a
sling, having been wounded at the battle of Châtil-
lon, at which few of "The Sons of Brutus," it was
reported, had thought it necessary to appear.

These three persons were the sole relict of the
congregation of Ste. Rosamonde: everybody else had
fled—they only remained: and when I say that they
remained, I should be speaking more truly if I said
that what remained of them was the ghost of their
former selves. Yes, only the ghost, for these were
certainly not the people I had known before. What
was there in common, for instance, between the
Countess of Verveine of last summer, the young,
high-born, lovely, courted millionaire widow, who was
looked up to—worshipped would be the better word
—as one of the queens of *ton*, and this pale, large-
eyed young woman in the Sister of Mercy's dress
who was patiently mending a bullet-hole in a tunic
belonging to a wounded soldier? And young
Robache, what had come over him? The last time
I had seen him was at Longchamps at the running
for the Grand Prize, in June. Blooming in a white
waistcoat, straw-coloured gloves, moss-rose bud, and
inseparable eye-glass, he had driven down on his
drag, the showiest turn-out of the field, betted heavily
on Sornette, the French horse, and on seeing the
object of his predilections pass the post first, danced

a hornpipe *coram populo*, shaken everybody by the hand, and told me twenty times in five minutes that Waterloo was now at length avenged, since the British steed had been defeated. What relation was this young madcap to the curiously gaunt individual I saw before me now, his head cropped close as a convict's, his private's uniform all too large for him, and his left arm closely bound to his chest by a combination of straps and bandages? As for M. Tricoche, he had aged five years between the 8th of May and the 4th of September; and between the 4th of September and my present visit it seemed to me that he had aged five years more. The only point in which there was no perceptible alteration in any of the three was in their natural serenity. They were thin, half-starved, fatigued, but for all that the national characteristics asserted their sway and they were cheerful. I even doubt if they ever took a deeper interest in any of their past occupations than in those to which they were devoting themselves at the moment when I entered.

They sat round a deal table outside the extemporized pharmacy. Young Robache, whose wound allowed of his making himself useful, in so far as one hand went, was holding one end of a piece of linen between his teeth, the other end being fastened to the table's edge, and was gravely scraping lint with a knife. The Curé, with a heap of letters on one side of him, large sheets of postage-stamps on the other, was franking missives he had written by request of wounded soldiers to their relatives, correspondence destined for the provinces, and to be forwarded by the next balloon. Mdme. de Verveine, as I have said, was all absorbed in her needlework, and on a chair beside her towered a pile of other tunics and jackets waiting to be attended to when that which she had in hand was finished. She looked up, however, as I advanced, walking on tiptoe so as not to wake anybody. I bowed to her, she smiled with her usual grace, and said in a hushed voice—

"Colonel de Kerhoel has been here this morning. He says you sent him here to protect us. Do you know we were rather alarmed at first, not for us, but for our patients? Do you think there is any real danger?"

"Not now, certainly, thanks to Colonel de Kerhoel; but I should have been sorry to receive the visit of these gentlemen without him."

"Why, what can they want?" asked the Curé simply.

"Want, Monsieur le Curé" echoed the surgeon, joining us and laughing quietly. "Why, what those gentlemen have wanted ever since I have had the pleasure of knowing them—and our acquaintance dates from the Revolution of 1848—I never knew them desire but two things: Do no work, and pay themselves out of the pockets of other people for doing it."

"Perhaps they are hungry, and that would excuse a great deal of desperation," rejoined the Countess, gently. "I assure you it quite makes my heart bleed to read of the prices of things in the papers. See here what the *Journal des Débats* says: 'Butter, 80 francs the pound; fowls, 40 francs the pair; a cabbage, 3 francs; eggs, 90 centimes apiece.' What the poor are to do I cannot think."

"Yes, I saw a poor woman yesterday, a small tradesman's wife, trying to get a cup of milk for her child, who was ill," remarked the Curé, gloomily. "There was not a drop to be had in the quarter— at least not for the price she could afford."

"So you went and bought it for her," added the surgeon, concluding the sentence which the worthy Curé would certainly have left unfinished. "Yes, no doubt the poor are to be pitied, but the poor at this moment are not those whom Mdme. la Comtesse supposes. Those who before the siege called themselves the 'working-men' are as well off now as they have ever been in their lives, in fact a great deal better off. They have no rent to pay, they are ab-

solved from all their debts till the end of the war,
they have warm clothes given them gratis, and they
receive 30 sous a day, with fifteen added if they be
married men. But this is not all. Thanks to the
municipal canteen, which the Government has in-
stituted, they live almost for nothing. Their dinners
are sumptuous beside yours, Madame, who refuse to
eat anything better than what they give the soldiers,
and yours, M. le Curé, who live on bread and horse.
For eight sous they are entitled to a large bowl of
soup, their ration of cooked meat, a plate of beans
or potatoes, half-a-pound of bread, and half a litre
of wine, and they may go and take two meals of
this sort a day. So you see, those who are suffering from hunger, and are likely to die of the com-
plaint if the siege lasts much longer, are not the
'down-trodden proletaries,' as these gentlemen love to
call themselves. No, those who are hungry now,
who have changed places with the beggars, are the
unfortunate petty *bourgeois*, the small tradesmen, the
ten thousand subaltern *employés* who in peace-time
had to keep up a rag of respectability, and who at
present must choose between paying for their cabbages three francs apiece, or going without cabbages
and living on that mouthful of horse which the
Government allows. A good many of these poor
devils have become very scarecrows. I saw one of

them last week—they told me he was a railway clerk—go and take up his post outside one of the municipal canteens, along with his *queue*, waiting for the distribution. He probably thought that, being starving, he had as much right to some soup as any other citizen. But you should have seen the storm his coming excited. He was recognized by a neighbour, and set upon by the whole concourse, tooth and nail, beak and claw. What! a man who used to have three thousand francs a year beg for soup! An 'aristocrat' come and snatch the bread out of the People's mouth! In less than a twinkling he was felled into the gutter, his jug kicked out of his hand, his vile aristocratic body pummelled into a jelly, and it was lucky for him that the canteen doors were opened just at this juncture, else I doubt if he would have remained in a position ever to feel hungry again. Ah, they are pleasant gentlemen, these down-trodden proletaries, when you take the muzzle off them."

"Dear me, dear me, this is all very dreadful," said the Countess, "but if these men are not hungry what can they want with us? I suppose it is some of these terrible politics again," added she, with a sigh.

"Humph! politics! I would willingly give a hundred-franc note to any Son of Brutus who explained to me what he understood by that word, and another hundred if he told me frankly what his ideal of a good government was," answered the surgeon, sceptically. "They have got a Republic now, and they are conscientiously doing their utmost to upset it; if they ever install themselves in its place under the name of double-dyed or treble-dyed Republic, you may depend upon their clutching each other by the throat, even as they have done on every former occasion, when it has pleased Providence to give them their turn at the helm. As for what they say about the Bonapartists bringing on this war, you know what my opinion is respecting that, Madame, and so do you, M. le Curé."

"Yes, yes, my dear doctor, I know you are indulgent," answered the Curé, sighing.

"Not indulgent, but just," answered the surgeon, plainly. "If I thought that this war was due to any particular party, I should say so; but my conviction is, that it was a fatality in which we all had a hand, without exception. As an old soldier who has served under the Dukes of Nemours and Aumale, I have always been an Orleanist; but I, too, was a partisan of this war, so was every Frenchman worth his salt; and if a few held back, I own I cannot rid myself of the notion that politics had more to do with it than love of peace. Had the Government backed out of their war-scrape whilst it was yet time, I would have wagered a good deal that the Republican party-cry henceforth would have been that the Emperor was afraid to fight the Prussians."

"Well, well," rejoined the Curé, gravely, "let us be just to every man according to his works. The Republicans acted rightly in opposing the war: I prefer to think that their motives were good."

I am unable to guess what reply, if any, the surgeon would have made, for whilst the Curé was speaking, a distant clamour, as of an adjoining crowd, reached our ears; and he had scarcely done, when one of the ambulance attendants ran in scared, and said: "There is an enormous mob of National Guards and workmen; they are carrying red flags, and shouting, '*A bas les Prêtres de Rosemonde!*' and they are coming down the street!"

IV.

It was quite true. There they were, an enormous mob, shaggy, turbulent, and in excellent spirits for mischief. The Citizen Bilia had originally projected a purely civilian demonstration, but those second thoughts which the proverb assures us are best, had counselled him to admit his armed battalion of National Guards to a participation; and so they

6*

trooped behind him, five hundred strong, draggle-
tailed, undisciplined, and singing patriotic songs,
furiously out of tune, as became true Republicans,
averse to any sort of order or regulation. This, by
the way, was the eleventh or twelfth "demonstration,"
in which the Citizen Bilia's battalion took part. It
was always demonstrating, this valuable cohort of
warriors. One day it was trudging processionally
through the mud to crown a statue somewhere;
another day it went in state to howl at the Government at the Hôtel-de-Ville; a third day it would go
and sack somebody's house, for the greater glory of
the good cause; and so on. Perhaps it will seem to
certain minds that, considering the Prussians were
knocking rather importunately at the gates of Paris,
the Citizen Bilia's battalion might have found a
more useful field for its energies in endeavouring to
induce the Prussians to go away. But to this I answer that, if every man did his duty, there would
soon be nothing to complain of: not even war, for
instance, which would be a pity, seeing how lucrative
a trade it is becoming; nor revolutions, which would
be a most painful blow to such gentlemen as the
Citizen Bilia.

I think that Citizen Bilia had counted upon an
agreeable morning's sport; and this will account for
the singularly wry face he pulled when, upon de-

bouching into the Place de Ste. Rosemonde, he found himself confronting not an unguarded place of worship, but eight hundred soldiers, neatly drawn up in square, and armed with Chassepot rifles.

Colonel de Kerhoel had marshalled his men in such a way as to leave a clear road for any person or body of persons whose object was simply to pass by the church, but also in such a way as to oppose a simple, solid, thoroughly unengaging barrier to anybody who ruminated an attack. The experienced eye of Citizen Bilia took in all this at a glance. He was no fool; no more were his men, for they, too, seemed struck by the practical character of the arrangements. However, for the dignity of the thing they kept on advancing neither did they in any marked degree abate their howlings. These howls were a trifle less enthusiastic, that was all; and when they were all opposite the church together, they halted. The two hosts then stood face to face.

One might well have drawn some moral from the contrast they offered. It was the contrast between those old irreconcilable enemies, Provincial France and the Capital. On one side these Bretons —a rough lot, dogged, ignorant, far from clean, and speaking no language but their own rude *patois*, sturdy churls, nevertheless, Catholics to the core, believers in amulets, singers of wild, superstitious hymns, and devoted to their God, their priest, and their legitimate chief with a fidelity it would have been as impossible to shake as one of those rugged rocks by their own seashore. On the other hand, this mob of Parisians—dirty and ignorant as the countrymen, but believing in nothing and respecting nobody, ready with a grin and a lampoon for everything that was law, order, religion, or morality, and grinning behind the back even at that trumpery leader of theirs whom, a moment's freak, they had set up to guide them, and whom, whenever the fancy took them, they would break as unceremoniously as an ape does a nut.

The Parisians looked at the Bretons as bumptious townsmen look at peasants. The Bretons returned the glance as a bull-dog eyes a cat—able to strangle him, and not reluctant to do it.

The mere exchange of glances was not of long duration, for Colonel de Kerhoel, in a peremptory but off-hand tone, gave the word of command: "Attention! Fix bayonets!"

The Citizen Bilia, not to be behindhand, instantly sang out, in a piercing falsetto, "ATTENTION! FIX BAYONETS!"

The next move was the Colonel's, who took out a cigar and lit it. The Citizen Bilia felt in his pockets, but finding no cigar, did nothing, and there

was a pause. But only for a minute. Impelled by
the vociferations of "The Sons of Brutus," who, re-
garding the cigar as a token of pacific intentions,
waxed noisy and sanguine anew, the Citizen Bilia
stepped forward, and, in a voice which he meant to
be haughtily defiant, but which quavered slightly in
his throat, shouted: "Citizen Colonel, in the name
of the Republic one and indivisible, we summon the
Citizens Tricoche and Robache, and the Citoyenne
Verveine, to appear before us."

"Monsieur le Commandant," replied the Colonel
politely, "the persons you mention are unknown to
me. I have the honour of being acquainted with
Madame la Comtesse de Verveine, Monsieur l'Abbé
Tricoche, Curé of Ste. Rosemonde, and with· Monsieur Robache; but they are at this moment engaged,
and you will excuse me if I decline interrupting them
for the sake of announcing your visit."

"*Oh, là là!*" "*Plus de Saints!*" "*A bas les
aristocrates et les porteurs d'eau bénite!*" "*A Chaillot les
Comtesses!*" yelled the gentlemen in the background.

"Citizen Colonel," pursued the Commandant
Bilia, making heroic efforts to surmount the lump
which was rising in his gullet, "you hear the wishes
of the people. I am their delegate. I call upon
you to let me pass."

"I must trouble you to stand back," replied the Colonel simply.

"And if I refuse—if I insist upon advancing?"

The Colonel quietly unsheathed his sword. "I shall cleave you in two like a carrot," said he.

But the precious blood of the Citizen Bilia was not destined to flow, for a hand was laid on the Colonel's arm, and Madame de Verveine, who had come out of the church with M. Tricoche, young Robache, the surgeon, and myself, interposed:—"You desire to see me, monsieur?" she said to M. Bilia.

The Citizen Commandant was not able immediately to answer, for the disagreeable menace of Colonel de Kerhoel had a little unsettled him. The fact is, he was not used to be talked to in this way. When he went "demonstrating" before the Government offices, things passed off quite differently. An official secretary, not unfrequently a Minister in person, came down to listen to his observations, and he was always assured that the Government would give his remarks their most attentive consideration, and every disposition was shown not to ruffle his feelings or in any manner irritate him. He scarcely knew what to think of this new form of proceeding—this promise to cleave him in two,—a threat which was the more offensive as there was not the slightest reason to suppose M. de Kerhoel would not put it into execution.

However, at the sight of Madame de Verveine, he rallied. He had doubtless heard that in the sphere in which Colonel de Kerhoel moved it was customary for male aristocrats to contain themselves before female aristocrats. So, feeling himself safe, he drew his sword, brandished it above his head, and darting glances of unquenchable fury, holloaed:— "Who is it that threatens me? I dare you to do your worst! The people have resolved that the ambulances where our brothers are lying shall no longer be sullied by the persons of the Second Empire. We will have no more Jesuits, and no more he or she comedians . . . ." ("*No no*," roared the gentlemen behind. "*No more Jesuits*.")

"I assure you, you will not find any brother of yours yonder," remarked the surgeon ironically. "All the men in that ambulance are soldiers; there is not a single ragamuffin among them."

"Tush, tush!" pleaded worthy M. Tricoche. "I am sorry M. le Commandant, that our presence should be a source of annoyance to any one," added he, with imperturbable gentleness. "It is but too true that I am one of those who, at the outset of this unlucky war, spoke otherwise than they ought to have done, —otherwise, I may add, than became my character as a priest; and I shall not think I have done enough even when I have devoted my entire fortune and the energies of my whole life to remedying some of the evils which I have helped to occasion. So if there is any particular form of expiation, monsieur, which you wish to suggest to me in the name of public opinion, I will pray in all humility for grace to submit to it."

"Excuse me one moment," said young Robache, coming forward. "Before favouring us with his scheme of expiations, M. Bilia will perhaps do well to consider to what extent it will have to be put in practice by himself. How do you do, M. Bilia? I have never had the opportunity of making your personal acquaintance, but it has been given me to peruse a document of your composition; and as the byword says that the style marks the man, I should be almost justified in saying that we are acquainted."

The Citizen Bilia turned sallow, and stared with evident uneasiness at the close-cropped youth whose eyeglass gleamed upon him with the disconcerting fixity of a policeman's lantern.

"Yes, it was a letter sent to my father, then a Minister—a Minister of the Second Empire. Whilst he was in office he received a good many such epistles. I confess they were not characterized for the most part by excess of dignity, but one day he lit upon one which for flatness and servility exceeded anything he had ever fingered before, and he showed it me as a curiosity. The author states his wish to serve that poor Second Empire anyhow and anywhere, as a sub-prefect, a sub-receiver, a clerk of the préfecture de police, 'in any capacity, in short, where he could prove his devotion towards that august dynasty whose coming had been as that of the blessed manna from heaven.' I remember the very words, they struck me as infinitely poetic. I am glad to perceive, M. le Commandant, that the rejection of this petition—which you will have no difficulty in recollecting was signed 'Christophe Bilia'—has not prevented your making your way in another walk."

"It's a calumny!" gasped the Citizen Bilia, become livid: "a base, hireling calumny." · And the gentlemen in the background, beginning to wonder what the conversation could be about, caught at the cry, and shouted all together, with cordial waving of red flags and shaking of fists: "*Yes, yes, it's a calumny; don't believe them. A bas les calomniateurs!*"

"Well, well," continued young Robache, "a short memory is no crime; but let us come to another subject, that of this war, which you are good enough to lay on our shoulders. On the 15th of July last —you see I am precise about my dates—I was driving down the Rue St. George towards seven in the evening. That day M. Thiers—you know M. Thiers?—had made a speech in the Corps Législatif in favour of peace, and a deputation of the sovereign people were marking their grateful sense of the proceeding by putting some stones through his windows. There was one gentleman distinguishing himself particularly in this exercise. He was better dressed than the others, and appeared to be leading them; he moreover shouted, '*A Berlin!   A mort les Allemands!   A bas les pacifiques!*' with a zeal that did him credit. Somehow, M. Bilia I would stake my word of honour that this gentleman was yourself."

The Citizen Bilia's first impulse was apparently to renew his protestations with redoubled scorn, but a better mode of tactics presented itself to his imagination. Drawing himself up to his full height of five feet three or thereabouts, he hurled out the indignant cry of the fox who has set a trap and fallen into it himself: "Citizens," shrieked he, "we have got into an ambush. Let us have nothing to say to these people who lie in wait to slaughter Republicans. Citizen Colonel, I call all here present to witness that you have threatened my life, and that had I not been actuated by the most patriotic forbearance, a conflict might have ensued between us.

Citizens, let us withdraw. It shall not be said that whilst the enemy is at the gates we allowed ourselves to be provoked into civil strife. If these people wish to enter into rivalry with us, they know where to find us. Let them follow us to the field of battle, and fight by our sides — if they dare." Hereupon he wheeled to the right about, put himself at the head of his men, gave the order to march, and strode off superbly. And his men followed him as before, not a little impressed by his eloquence, and reflecting that, after all, it would have been absurd to attack these Bretons, who were a low herd, imbued with degrading prejudices, and who, besides, would have been just as likely as not to rout them.

"Well, Madame," said the Colonel, sheathing his sword and smiling grimly, as the last Son of Brutus vanished, bawling with tremendous rage:—

> "Tremblez, ennemis de la France—
> Rois ivres de sang et d'orgueil;
> Le Peuple Souverain s'avance:
> Tyrans, descendez au cercueil!"—

"Well, Madame, all's well that ends well!"

"Heaven grant that it may all end well," answered she fervently, but with a sigh. "You cannot think," she added, mournfully, "what a sorrow it is to me that, at a time when we ought all to be united, there should be such enmities as these between fellow-countrymen. It is more cruel than the war itself."

The Colonel became suddenly grave.

"Ay," said he, bitterly, "and do you not think it rends my heart to pieces to think that the man I have just treated like a dog was a Frenchman? I could cry with shame at the thought. Yes, God knows how it will all end; but if you are beaten, my poor France, it is not the Krupp guns or the German generals that will have defeated you: your own children have hurt you more than all your foes together."

V.

Whither the Citizen Bilia betook himself upon leaving the Ambulance Tricoche, and whether he ever put into execution his threat of proceeding to the battle-field, in order to shame those dastard Bretons who had lain in wait to slay a Republican, are points which I am not in a position to clear up. But I am inclined to think that the Citizen Bilia did not visit the battle-field. A man cannot devote his mind to two things at once, and M. Bilia and friends found plenty to occupy them inside the city, without seeking for adventures out of doors. On the 31st of October they tried to overturn the Government, in the month of December they tried again, and on the 24th of January they made a third effort, not more successful than the other two, but more glorious in this respect, that it resulted in a certain number of deaths, which always reads well in newspaper accounts. By this time, however, M. Bilia had ceased to be a Commandant, having been despotically cashiered, as he feelingly expressed it: and his battalion had also been disbanded, and there were some unpleasant rumours that if the Government caught M. Bilia it intended shooting him, which I believe to have been a false report—for the Government of the National Defence would not have harmed a fly, not even a Prussian if it could have helped it—but which nevertheless had the effect of confining M. Bilia to out-of-the-way garrets, where he led an occult existence, only relieved by those occasional sorties to which I have just alluded. He reappeared altogether at the close of the siege, and I heard without surprise that he had been elected to represent an important democratical constituency in the National Assembly. There is a brilliant political future open before that young man. If he is fortunate enough to keep out of the hangman's hands there is no reason why he should not become Prime Minister, President of a Republic—Emperor, even, if the fancy takes him.

The fates of the other personages I have cursorily introduced were perhaps less enviable than that of the Citizen Bilia, perhaps more so, according to the point of view.   Colonel de Kerhoel was shot in that second attack on the Bourget with five hundred out of his eight hundred men.   Young Robache, not yet cured of his wound, but able to lift his arm sufficiently to hold a rifle, decamped from his ambulance without surgeon's leave, on the morning of the battle of Villiers, and was buried the next day in the small village churchyard, which was all too narrow to contain the number of French graves that had to be dug.   The surgeon himself was carried off by a stray shell whilst picking up the wounded on the field of Montretout; and at about the time of this, the last battle of the siege, I met with the following lines in the papers:—

" We regret to announce the death of Mdme. la Comtesse de Verveine, who died on the 15th, of typhus fever, caught in the Ambulance of Ste. Rosemonde, aged 28."

As for M. Tricoche, I had few occasions of speaking to him after the episode furnished by the visit of M. Bilia.   Our paths lay apart.   The duties of newspaper correspondence took me to all points of the compass, perpetually moving, perpetually scribbling; and if here and there, whilst jotting down notes at sunset on a corpse-strewn field, I caught sight of the well-known figure kneeling with gourd or crucifix in hand over a prostrate form, we

seldom either of us had more than the time to exchange a rapid word in passing or a silent grasp of
the hand. Still, I continued to hear of M. Tricoche.
Soldiers talked of him with a strange respect; generals wished there were a few more like him; Sons
of Brutus swore he was a Judas, and frequently
hooted him in the streets. I learned that his ambulance was always full, and it was cited as one of
those where the wounded enjoyed most luxuries; for
people said the Curé was spending every farthing
he had, and that of all the money he had put by as
Vicar of wealthy Ste. Rosemonde's, there would soon
be not a penny left. On the day when the peace
was signed I went to call upon M. Tricoche.

It was a sunshiny day. Paris seemed comparatively joyful—glad to know that the worst was over.
Everywhere people were beginning to reopen their
shops or unfasten their barricaded shutters; and in
front of Ste. Rosemonde's I found the Distinguished
Architect superintending the removal of the sacks
of earth off the pet work of his genius. The red-
cross flag was already gone, for it seems the
wounded had been removed to the military hospi-
tals, now less crowded. On the door figured this
new announcement:—

"*This Church will be reopened for Divine Service on the Sunday of
Mid-Lent.* "PIERRE CHAMBONNEAU, *Curé.*"

"Pierre Chambonneau!" said I, in astonishment, and addressing myself to the Distinguished Architect; "but what has become of M. Tricoche?"

"Oh, haven't you heard?" said my interlocutor, filliping an ash from his cigar and laughing. "M. Tricoche has resigned."

"Resigned? And for what reason?"

"Oh, you know"—and the Distinguished Architect shrugged his shoulders—"it's one of the new ideas that's come over him since the Empire fell. I can't say what's the meaning of it. I believe, myself, the good old man is a little—ahem!" (the D. A. touched his forehead). "Somebody has heard him pretend that having misled the congregation he was entrusted to guide, he deserves to be deprived of his office. They say the Archbishop tried to pacify him; but you know at that age, when they get any notion into their heads, it's the deuce and all to make them understand reason. M. Tricoche has obtained a place as Vicaire* in some wild, heaven-forsaken parish down in the Pyrenees.—I beg pardon. Heigh there! mind what you're about with that sack of earth: you all but sent it through the oriel."

I walked away, without a word, in the direction of M. Tricoche's lodgings. At the door a commissionaire was putting some luggage on a hand-truck,

* *Vicaire*, in French, is curate, and *curé*, vicar.

and Mdlle. Virginie, the Curé's housekeeper, dressed as if for a journey, was coming behind him, with a parcel or two.

"Oh, it's you, monsieur," said she, curtsying; "you're just in time to say good-bye to M. le Curé."

"Is it really good-bye?" I asked with some emotion: for the Curé just then appeared himself with the last of his luggage—a few books.

"Yes, dear friend," answered he, with a peaceful smile, and he held out his hand.

No doubt he guessed the mute question in my looks, for, still holding my hand, he said with quiet earnestness:—"*Lavabo inter innocentes manus meas; et invocabo misericordiam Domini.*" Then, making the sign of the cross before me as a farewell, he added:—"*Dominus tecum.*"

I am certain I never responded with deeper fervour:—"*Et cum spiritu tuo.*"

———

OUR FIRST SUCCESS.

OUR FIRST SUCCESS.

APROPOS OF DRAMATIC CENSORSHIP.

I.

THERE was not an author, journalist, or playwright in Paris but knew Monsieur Buche—"Monsieur Buche, de l'Académie Française," as he styled himself in his books; "le savant Monsieur Buche," as he was called by his friends; "the great Monsieur Buche," as he was derisively termed by a number of us good-for-nothing small fry, who were not ashamed to talk lightly of a person of his merit, but laughed at him, his works, and his bun-brown coat, as if he and his belongings were fit themes for jesting, instead of being the eminently staid, discreet, and venerable institutions they were.

Monsieur Buche—who was close upon seventy, and had always been close upon seventy ever since mankind could remember—Monsieur Buche had a collection of aphorisms, which he drew out from the recesses of his inner self as occasion served him,

l launched with majestuous gravity in the face of
rising generation. It was a solemn thing to hear
i ejaculate, "*caLumny*, I despise," laying a par-
ilar stress upon the letter *L*, as if to mark his
led conviction that calumny is not derived from
substantive *calumnia*, as certain among the
orant do vainly boast, but is a composite noun,
ned from the words *caleo*, to warm or to scald,
l *umnum*, contraction of *humanum* or *hominem*, an
illigent biped of the male gender. I have heard
i explain his theory on this subject with great
cision to two philosophers and a grammarian,
l, although the grammarian looked puzzled, I am
vinced M. Buche was in the right, for M. Buche
s unavoidably right in all that he said and did;
l if others did not think so, he himself always
., which is quite as conclusive, and every whit as
sfactory.

M. Buche was a Senator as well as an Academician,
l everybody seemed to think it perfectly proper
t he should be in the Senate, or, indeed, in any
er assembly where there was high pay to be had
l small work to be done. It is true that when
iple came to be asked what were M. Buche's
cial claims to sit in embroidered clothing and
islate for his fellows, they were often at a loss to
lain; but a good many got over the difficulty by

saying they supposed M. Buche was in the Senate because he was in the Academy — an excellent reason if ever there was one, for, as not a soul on earth knew why it was that M. Buche had been made an Academician, everybody was naturally afraid to ask, lest such a display of ignorance should draw down public contempt on the querist and cause him to be slighted and held up to contumely. The fact is, M. Buche was one of those men who make their way into the snug nooks and holes of the social edifice by the same mysterious but never-failing process which brings mice into the interstices of our dwelling-houses and well-fed spiders into the secret corners thereof. How come the mice there, and how the spiders, nobody can tell; and so it was with M. Buche. The only thing people knew for certain was, that so sure as ever there was a well-lined sinecure to be filled, or a cosy profit-yielding berth to be disposed of, so sure did the figure of the "savant M. Buche" loom upon the horizon with its bun-brown coat, gold-rimmed spectacles, stiff-starched gill-collar, and a look that seemed to say, "Who so fit as I to possess this sinecure? who so presumptuous as to question my right to it?" I hasten to remark that as a rule nobody ever did question the right of M. Buche either to the honours he possessed already, or to any others for which he might feel an appetite by-and-by. Once, to be sure, a miserable journalist—one of those degraded individuals who respect nothing—was ill-advised enough to hint that there might be no harm in inquiring what M. Buche had done that he should finger so much public money; but at this the outcry was so loud and general, and the words "envy," "slander," "malice," were so universally showered down, that the shameless writer was reduced to silence, M. Buche the while heaping coals of fire on his head by declaring with noble magnanimity that "he bore no rancour, for that the man was probably only an imbecile."

It was M. Buche who, at the Friday meetings of the Academy, was wont to read papers "on the decline of modern literature"—sorts of dirges in prose, uttered in tones of mournful grandeur and strenuously applauded by M. Buche's colleagues, many of whom understood not a word of what they heard, but of course clapped their hands the loudest so as not to be taken for simpletons. Now and then M. Buche would be induced to read one of these valuable papers in public, either in a drawing-room or lecture-room, and on such occasions it was a fine thing to watch the enthusiasm which his words excited amongst his audience. If the lecture was a paying one the tickets fetched a premium, and from the

moment when M. Buche stood up to the moment
when he sat down, one could hear on all sides such
exclamations as "Ah!" "Hear, hear!" "How true!"
"Admirable!" or, especially from certain old ladies
who dabbled in literature, and were not so keenly
appreciated by a short-sighted public as, by their
own demonstration, they should have been. There
were several popular journalists and authors, too,
who attended M. Buche's lectures; and it has more
than once occurred to me to observe the attitude of
these gentlemen whilst the Academician was in-
veighing with stern indignation against the flippancy
of modern literature. I avow with humility that I
myself am no judge of literature, for, to my unen-
lightened mind, many of these popular writers had
more talent in their little finger's end than M. Buche
in his whole person, bun-brown coat included; and
I would have given a great deal to see one of them
get up and call M. Buche a worn-out mummy, or
offer to fight him, or do something equally scandalous.
But, I repeat, this only proves the perverse and benighted state of my intellect. The popular authors,
who were better bred than I, usually took their
castigation very meekly. When M. Buche frowned
at novels and shrugged his shoulders at newspapers,
when he talked of journalism "as the idle occupation
of frivolous minds," and described novelists as "men

who entice the public from the healthy pabulum of
sound literature by the culpable allurements of un-
substantial fiction;" when he said all this and a good
deal besides, wielding the rod as if he had been
specially delegated by Providence to perform this
duty; I vow it upon my word there was not a soul
who laughed; nay, more, I am persuaded of this,
that if anybody had stood up and proclaimed aloud
that M. Buche himself had once written a novel, the
whole first edition of which was still lying untouched
upon the shelves at his publisher's, there would have
been a unanimous hooting, and the libeller would
have been hustled and ignominiously thrust out by
the neck and bowled into the gutter.

Naturally, M. Buche was an Imperialist, and had
been so ever since the 2nd December, 1851. He
voted with the Right (that is, with the majority) as
a matter of principle, and seldom missed the opportunity of introducing some of his pet aphorisms upon
the decline of contemporary literature into the speeches
he delivered from the tribune. It was currently reported, however, that once upon a time M. Buche had
been a liberal, a mild liberal according to some, an
out-and-out radical-republican according to others.
There were even a few who went the length of asserting that it was mainly owing to his presumed
liberalism that M. Buche had been able to make

such excellent head-way when he first started on his career. But this liberalism—even if true—was a thing so far distant, and the memory of it so extremely distasteful to M. Buche, that all right-minded people were agreed in covering it carefully over and avoiding allusions to it. Enough was it, for the present, that M. Buche was a Bonapartist, and likely to remain so until there was a change of dynasty. The rest concerned nobody. As M. Buche himself said in one of his remarkable speeches, "*il n'y a que les sots, Messieurs, qui ne changent jamais. Moi-même j'ai changé; mais en tout état de cause je puis me vanter de ceci:* QUE JE SUIS TOUJOURS RESTÉ DU BON CÔTÉ." And this was indeed true, for whatever else might be reported of M. Buche, nobody could gainsay that throughout every change of wind and weather he had always remained on the paying side.

II.

Now, after all that precedes, it will surprise nobody to hear that, in addition to numerous other posts he held, M. Buche had been appointed by Government to the exceedingly delicate and difficult functions of State Censor. As M. Buche notoriously abominated what he called modern novels, and detested still more, if possible, anything that resembled

a modern play, successive Ministers had wisely decided that he was the fittest person to judge of such
works impartially. I may remark, in passing, that it
is this luminous spirit of discrimination in the choice
of candidates for important posts which has served
to make the name of Government so extremely
popular in our country, and secured us that happy
immunity from revolution which we have enjoyed
during the present century. M. Buche was one of
twenty, every bit as competent as himself, who met
together two or three times a week, either all together or in batches, to hold a sort of Pie-powder
Court over the literary productions of their contem-
poraries. Imagine a score of most antique and
venerable stage-coaches assembled to judge the per-
formances of some modern bicycles, and you will
have an accurate idea of the jurisprudence to be got
out of this model tribunal. So long as only novels
were concerned, the Censors were indulgent enough:
for at most they could only refuse to grant the
*estampille** to a book; and this, as they were pro-

---

* Unless a book has received the *estampille* (stamp) of the Censorship,
it can neither be sold within railway-stations, nor be hawked about the
country by pedlars. At first sight it might seem that the refusal of
the stamp must be a death-blow to any work; but the contrary is the
case. If the Censorship decline to stamp a book, as being immoral or
subversive, the publisher generally sells three or four editions within the
first month.

bably aware, was rather an advantage than otherwise
to the author. But when they were met to examine
a play it was another matter; and they might then
be seen in their glory. Neither genius, nor talent,
nor reputation found favour in their sight. Emile
Augier and Victor Hugo, young Dumas and Sardou,
George Sand and Barrière, all shared the common
lot. Ah, ah! talent and reputation indeed! What
were talent and reputation to twenty old gentlemen
armed with red-chalk pencils and eager to show their
zeal on behalf of public morality? The only possible chance that an author could have of getting off
unscathed was to confine his plot strictly to the
harmless topics of seduction and adultery, elopement
and murder; but if, in an evil moment, a dramatist
so far forgot himself as to transgress these bounds
and to talk of politics or social reforms—Oh, oh! it
was then that the Censors bridled up with their
scissors and pencils; cutting out this passage and
blurring that, glaring with indignant eyes upon the
culprit and crying out in scandalized tones about
the profligacy of the present age, and the necessity
of safeguarding the public against insidious forms
of contamination.

. No wonder that, with such intelligent Censors to
watch over us, the morals of my countrymen should
be so pure, and that the French stage especially,

should be so universally noted for everything that is proper, exemplary, and pleasant!

I am coming now to the subject of my narrative. As you may suppose, I have not been at such pains to introduce M. Buche for the simple pleasure of telling you that he habitually wore a bun-brown coat, and that his maxim upon things in general was, "Keep to the weather side." M. Buche may have been a great man, greater than anybody else in the whole French Empire; but his very existence might perhaps have remained unknown to me had it not been for the unpleasant fact that I was one day brought into contact with him—brought into contact as the earthenware pot in the fable was with the iron pot, very considerably to its damage and not a little to its mortification.

I must tell you that I have a friend named Théodore Trémolin who writes poetry. Wherefore Trémolin should write poetry is a mystery, for it doesn't pay him, and there are many other trades, such as shoe-blacking or knife-grinding, which he might exercise with greater profit to himself and more advantage to the community. But be this as it may, Trémolin writes poetry, and has done so ever since he was turned loose from school, six or seven years ago, with his head stuffed full of Horace, and his boxes crammed with prize-books, *proxime accesserunts* on

vellum, and other trophies of a liberal education.
The publishers of Paris know Trémolin, and duck
down side-streets when they descry him on the
Boulevards. He has a shock head of hair, pockets
bulging out with manuscript, boots that go *clip-clap*
when they touch the pavement, and a general air of
being out-at-elbows and ravenous. Judged by the
canons of respectability which have force of law
amongst grocers, cheesemongers, and people who pay
their rent, Trémolin would be set down as a repro-
bate, for he never has a sou in his pocket, sleeps
where he can, dines only on gala-days, and jokes at
constituted authorities. This last propensity is a
fatal one, for it makes nine-tenths of the population
avoid Trémolin like a mad dog. What security can
there be, indeed, in the presence of an individual
who does not see the use of a municipal councillor,
and laughs at a mayor as at something grotesque
and fantastic? You English have only to imagine a
person addicted to joking at vestrymen to sympathize
heart and soul with those orderly Parisians who
classed Trémolin somewhat higher than an assassin,
but infinitely lower than a pickpocket.

Well, as this black sheep was a friend of mine,
it was only natural that he should end by imparting
to me a taste for some of his evil practices, and one
bright morning I was astonished to find that he and

I had been living six months together; lodging in a kind of garret close under the roof on the sixth floor, and writing plays which we carried furtively to managers' letter-boxes and dropped in surreptitiously when it was dark and we were sure there was nobody looking. Trémolin was for high art, and would have had me write tragedies; for, though he himself was always laughing from one year's end to the other, his literary mood was essentially lugubrious, and it was seldom that his heroes escaped death by strangulation. But on this point my personal experience stood me in good stead. I had had three tragedies in five acts refused at the Odéon, and was consequently able to assure Trémolin that contemporary managers were wanting in taste for the higher branches of the drama. I cannot say that this greatly intimidated Trémolin; for being of a bold turn of mind, he would have cheerfully persevered, all managers and friends notwithstanding. But he showed himself amenable to reason, and, on being properly indoctrinated, agreed to write extravaganzas, which, as he sagaciously remarked, were often mere tragedies with the frame changed. "You see," said he, "it will be considered a very funny thing if I hang half my people in the last act of a burlesque, and as for the speeches of my *dramatis personæ*, *King Lear* and *Cinna* might be turned into first-rate farces if you only set the declamations to music and intercalated break-downs at the pathetic bits."

After a time, however, it became manifest even to Trémolin that the art of bread-making and that of verse-making have no sort of direct analogy, and that there is perhaps on the whole a good deal to be said for the knife-grinding trade, in which a man may earn two-and-sixpence a day and go to sleep at night with a quiet conscience. I can guess what it must have cost Trémolin to arrive at this conclusion, for he would rave about Art for hours without stopping, and often vowed, with a hand on his waistcoat, that he would cleave to this mistress so long as he had a crust of bread left. But here was just the point; for after six months in our garret we neither of us had crusts of bread; and all the respectable people of the neighbourhood, our landlord included, spoke of us as a pair of lazy stay-at-home vagabonds, who ought to be set to break stones to learn what hard work was. One day poor Trémolin, who had been looking at me ruefully for a few minutes, threw down his pen and said, with a shrug of the shoulders, "This beats me, Victor; I see it won't do! I vote we go and enlist."

It was about seven o'clock in the evening, and from our window on the sixth floor we could hear

the rumbling of a long line of carriages drawn up
outside the Senate, where his Excellency the President was giving a grand dinner-party. We were in
early spring: the sun was just setting over Paris; and
as we got up and looked down the street, leaning
side by side against the window-sill, we could descry,
like small dots on the pavement below, a fine
sprinkling of comfortable citizens taking their evening airing with that leisurely gait peculiar to men
who have eaten and are filled. By a stretch of
imagination we fancied we could see the faces of
the Senators, Ambassadors, Ministers, and Deputies,
who were going to his Excellency's banquet. They,
too, seemed comfortable, and replete by anticipation.
As M. Buche was a Senator, he of course was among
the guests, but we did not know him then, and so
could take no note of his bun-brown brougham with
his bun-brown horses and its brown-clad coachman,
all as solemn and magnificent as it behoved the belonging of such a master to be. It was an exasperat-
ing thing, however, to look at so many people who
had already dined, and so many more who were
about to dine, and yet to feel, as Trémolin put it,
that our own hopes of future dinners were based
upon contingencies as slender as a needle's point.
"I have been reflecting," remarked my friend, with
a grumble, "that you and I have both lighted on

bad times, Victor." And saying this, he emptied the remainder of his tobacco-pouch into his pipe and began to smoke musingly. "You see if we had been born five hundred years ago we should not have talked about remaining dinnerless. If we had had no dinner of our own we should have walked into a house and taken somebody else's dinner, and the thing would have seemed rather a good joke than otherwise to the public at large. As for the owner of the dinner, the question to debate with him would have been not one of equity but of fists. You would have fought him, I should have looked on to see fair play, and after you had established your supremacy I should have eaten my share of the dinner and cried *Væ victis?* If your adversary had behaved remarkably like a brick throughout the whole affair, we should, perhaps, have thrown him the bones of his own banquet, and so gained a character for chivalry. At the conclusion of the entertainment, when we had cleared out the last platter, and turned the wine-gourds upside down to see that there was nothing left in them, I should have drawn out my tablets and written a rhythmical account of our achievement, which we should have gone about singing from castle to castle, mandolin in hand, thus earning other dinners, to say nothing of a reputation as very admirable fellows and clever

wags to boot. Those were good times. Nowadays
we have a civilization which leaves us dinnerless,
and an excellent code of laws which forbids us to
take our neighbour's dinner. Of course the neighbour, feeling his dinner protected, by the omnipotent
vigilance of these laws, would see us both hanged
before he would give us a mouthful, and if we were
to dispense with his leave and take his dinner by
force, after throwing him out of the window, no
amount of rhyming on our part could ever induce
a magistrate to believe that we were nothing more
than modern Plantagenets or Montmorencys following in the footsteps of our ancestors. This proves,
O Victor—and yet why are you named Victor, since
you are unable to conquer a dinner?—this proves, I
say, that, in proportion as humanity grows rich in
steam-ploughs and municipal councillors, its sense of
the humorous becomes blunted, its views as to right
and wrong become narrowed, and its respect for
poets dwindles to so mean a level that it suffers
Théodore Trémolin to go to bed supperless."

Théodore had got so far in his monologue when
there was a knock at the door, which brought him
abruptly to a standstill. It was a harsh knock, quick
and hard.

"Ah!" said he tragically, "a creditor! Shout to
him that we are not at home."

But it was not a creditor. The door opened and in walked la Mère Thérèse, wife of the *concierge*, bringing a letter.

"O most ancient and revered matron," cried Théodore, relieved, "what message is it that thou bearest in thy saffron fingers? Is it the petition of a creditor? If so, haste thee with a pen and write to say that the house of Trémolin and Marmelot have long suspended payment. Is it a missive of love? If so, O matron, then use a milder strain, and tell the fair one that *malesueta Fames* and *turpis Egestas* have driven an *æs triplex circum hæc duo pectora*. Or is it rather an invitation to dine at the table of the great in the company of the high-born and illustrious? Ah! matron, I have thee there: if such be the tenour of the despatch thou bringest, then out with thy best sheet of paper and thy most florid style, and say to the patrician who has asked these two poets to dinner, that in a certain office of the Mount of Piety two dress-coats lie in bondage awaiting an usurious ransom; and that never—no, never —so long as these coats are in captivity, will the sons of the Muses consent to be hospitably entertained in the halls of the magnates of this empire."

Mère Thérèse did not seem much impressed by these eloquent adjurations. "Leave off that silly talk, now do," she exclaimed, indignantly, and deposited the letter on the table amidst a heap of manuscripts and unfinished lyrics. After this she marched out as she had come, and left us to our reflections.

When we were alone again Théodore Trémolin and I stood for a moment silent, looking at the letter. We had both drawn near the table, and Théodore had stopped laughing. He was doing his best to seem unconcerned, but the glances he cast at the little square piece of paper in the centre of the table were too wistful for real indifference. Why is it that we appear to guess, by the sight of certain envelopes, whether the letter within brings good news or bad? This envelope looked like good news, but we had been disappointed so often that we were afraid to break the seal.

"You open it," began Théodore; "I have not the pluck to."

"Nor I," I rejoined.

"Well, then, let us draw lots," said he. "Fate will choose the boldest."

We drew lots. The lot fell on me, and with nervous slowness I opened the letter. It contained what follows:—

Théâtre des Fantaisies Comiques, Paris.

THE Manager of the Théâtre des Fantaisies Comiques presents his compliments to MM. Théodore Trémolin and Victor Marmelot, and begs they will do him the favour to be present at the theatre at two o'clock to-morrow, to read their three-act extravaganza, *Ptolomée XXIII., ou is Bœuf à l'Huile.*

III.

The next day, at two o'clock in the afternoon, the green-room of the Théâtre des Fantaisies Comiques was crowded to hear the reading of a new piece by two young gentlemen, whose names the stage porter announced as MM. Semolina and Marmalade. Both young gentlemen being profoundly unknown to fame, there was a buzz of curiosity and a whispering behind fans as the two walked in and looked shyly around them for somebody to speak to. At one end of the room sat a young lady with a fine red chignon and a dress of pale blue silk, play-ing with a curly white dog like a ball of fluff, and listening absently to the conversation of two or three gentlemen, with flowers in their button-holes and straw-coloured gloves on their hands. As the Théâtre des Fantaisies Comiques prided itself upon being an essentially aristocratic house, MM. Semolina and Marmalade took these well-dressed gentlemen for actors, and felt not a little ashamed of their own costumes—which had, alas! been hired for the oc-casion of one of those providential Hebrews who let out dress-suits at five francs the night, and wedding-

garments at ten francs fifty centimes the day. In
a recess, somewhere behind the lady in blue, a couple
of other gentlemen, robust and well-to-do, were
smoking cigarettes and exchanging remarks in a
confidential whisper, appearing to take no notice of
a young lady in mauve who was pinning strips of
paper to their coat-tails. A third young lady, in
cerise, had got a cigarette between her teeth, like
the two portly gentlemen, and seemed to enjoy it
amazingly. The rest of the figures present offered
only a confused jumble of silks and ribbons, high
hats and frock-coats, faces shaven and faces rouged,
hair flowing over the shoulders and hair piled up in
rolls, fans and parasols, umbrellas and walking-canes,
eyeglasses single and eyeglasses double, Havannah
dogs and King Charles' spaniels, patchouli and
musk, eau-de-Cologne and millefleurs: the whole of
which ingredients blended together constituted a
dozen members of both sexes, who were all talking
aloud about every conceivable subject, from politics
and horse-racing down to vaccination and the price
of truffles. In the centre of the room stood a table
with two blotting-books, two pens, an inkstand, two
chairs, a sugar-basin, a decanter of water, and a
couple of glasses.

"Ah!" exclaimed one of the two robust gentlemen, catching sight of Trémolin and me. Then ad-

vancing, he said politely, "Monsieur Marmalade, I believe?"

"Marmelot," I suggested.

"Ah, yes, to be sure. And this is Monsieur Semolenta, your friend? Well, I'm delighted to make your acquaintance. Your piece is funny—deuced funny. Where did you get your title from? You see I don't know how it is, but I'm no hand at titles, as I daresay you've noticed. When I've written a play I take it to my friend Langouste—that's Langouste down there with the yellow gloves talking to Mimi Triboulette—and it's he who finds me the title. A great hand at titles, Langouste. One day I took him a farce in two acts—devilish clever thing, though I say it—Langouste had got a toothache, and was as sulky as a bear. He wouldn't read the farce, declared it bored him; but at last, to get rid of me, he roared out, 'Is there anything about a drum in it?' 'Nothing,' I said. 'Is there anything about a trumpet?' 'Not a word,' said I. 'Well, then, call it *Sans Tambour ni Trompette*, and be hanged to you!' And so I did, by heaven! And the piece ran two hundred nights. Ha, ha! Diable de Langouste, va!"

At this juncture the stout gentleman descried one of the strips of paper which the young lady in mauve had pinned to his coat-tail, and proceeded to remove it.

"It's Zephirine who did that," he remarked, quietly. "Just be kind enough to dip your hand into my pocket, will you, and see if there's anything in it? Last week she put a pastepot there, and I don't want to be caught again. You've got no gloves on, so it doesn't matter. Of course you know Zephirine. No? Well, then, your friend M. Semolina does. What! you don't either? Ha! shouldn't have thought it possible. Well, come here and I'll introduce you."

I seized this occasion of putting in a word and thanking my stout interlocutor for his letter of the preceding day. He stopped short and stared at me.

"Egad!" he exclaimed, laughing, "you don't mean to say you took me for the lessee? Why, Masticot has got a face like a piece of putty cut into a conic section. It's a whole poem is that face of Masticot's. Imagine a countenance struggling to conceal the conflicting emotions of ambition and grim despair, and caught in the act by a pair of eyes which nature originally intended for an under-sized weasel. Masticot has been devoured all his life by one all-absorbing ambition—that of finding a hat to fit him; and the irremediable melancholy you will notice on his brow has been stamped there by a long succession of head-dresses, not one of which would ever allow the public to see aught of Masticot's face but the under lip and chin. Oh, no: I'm not Masticot! I'm only Masticot's friend. I hold his hat over his head for him when we walk down the Boulevards together, and so save him from premature death by extinction. But here is my card, Emile Javelin, at your service."

As everybody in civilized Europe knew Emile Javelin and his works, Trémolin and I both reddened together at my mistake. M. Javelin, however, appeared quite unoffended by it, and laying a hand patronizingly on each of our shoulders, pushed towards the lady in pale blue with the red chignon and the dog:—"Mademoiselle Mimi Triboulette and her dog," he said, introducing us. "You know, M. Marmalade, what Pericles said of his son's dog, Azor:—"Azor rules my boy, my boy rules his mother, his mother rules me, I rule Athens, Athens rules Greece, and Greece rules the world—wherefore Azor is the ruler of the world." Same remark applicable to Mdlle. Mimi Triboulette's dog, Bichon. Bichon governs Mdlle. Mimi, Mdlle. Mimi governs the Parisian public, the Parisian public governs Europe, Europe governs the two hemispheres —*ergo*, Bichon is the governor of the universe."

Mdlle. Mimi smiled and stroked the ears of Bichon, who eyed me contemptuously as an inter- loper, and showed his teeth at Trémolin. "Amiable dog, if ever there was one," continued M. Javelin: "he bit a piece out of a scene-shifter's leg the night before last; but I advise you to make friends with him, else his mistress will bear you a grudge, and sing all the best bits of your *Bœuf à l'Huile* out of tune. This, here in the cerise gown, is Mdlle. Sophie Mirabelle, who has hunted the fox in Eng- land, and rides at gates with five bars. The part of the young Fellah in the *Bœuf à l'Huile* will be for her. Sophie, my dear child, you belie the signi- fication of your name, which is Wisdom: if you per- sist in smoking cigarettes like that, you will end by blacking those pearl teeth of yours. Mdlle. Zephirine, here are two gentlemen who claim the honour of being introduced to you. Strip of paper pinned to coat-tail received and gratefully acknowledged by present speaker; I say this in passing. M. Semolina, I advise you to beware of Mdlle. Zephirine. She has broken the hearts of two stage managers, and hurried fifteen fiddlers out of the orchestra to an early grave. Her policy in life is never to learn her parts, and to sing the music as she fancies. There is a particular flute-player who has grown asthmatic from trying to keep pace with her. Those two gen-

tlemen with the geraniums are Counts de José and
de Nosé, two *habitués* who will view the first performance of the *Bœuf à l'Huile* from a stage-box,
and throw hundred-franc bouquets to Mdlle. Triboulette. Such noblemen are a godsend to the flower-
trade. For the rest of the company, *videte* playbill.
This on the right, with the pink necktie, is Claude
Doucette, the *tenorino*. 'Tis he will warble, 'Oh,
come to my heart, thou white-beaked swan,' in
Act i. scene 2. Further on, Alphonse Ballon, fami-
liarly *Boanerges*, the *basso-profondo*, who of course,
will be Raga-Muffin, the high-priest of Apis. There,
to the left, Grimaudin, the baritone, your future
Ptolomée XXIII., who will dance the *cancan* with
Mesdemoiselles Mimi and Zephirine, and cause
Counts de José and de Nosé to split their kid-gloves
with enthusiasm. Ha—ha! if I were a glover, I
would vote a statue to Counts de José and de Nosé.
But hullo! here we are. Right about face, young
gentlemen! this is M. Masticot and his *fidus Achates*,
Grosgoulu, the stage-manager.

The door had just opened and admitted two
gentlemen, the first of whom was of so small a size,
and looked so dejected under an overwhelmingly big
hat, that I supposed it must be the unfortunate M.
Masticot. His companion was also short, but made
up for this failing by being about three times the

mference of his superior. He was mopping a
:und visage with a voluminous pocket-hand-
iief, and exclaimed, "Ugh, how hot it is!" seven
; in the first ten minutes. Both gentlemen un-
red themselves on entering; and M. Masticot,
 a desponding nod, said, "Good afternoon,
s and gentlemen. I'm afraid I'm a little late.
Javelin, how do you do? I didn't expect to
you here. Where are the two authors? have
arrived yet?"

I. Emile Javelin pushed us forward both to-
:r, Trémolin and me; and the small M. Masti-
n the same glum tone as before, said,—"Thank
gentlemen, for being so punctual. I must con-
late you on your piece; I think it will do. We
it together the other night: and Grosgoulu here
ied at it, so did Javelin laugh at it; in fact,
all laughed at it. It is a very pleasant thing to
ble to laugh, gentlemen."

;rosgoulu here interposed: "It's a quarter to
;," said he, taking out his watch. "Suppose we
ı?"

Yes, yes, suppose we begin?" echoed the
ny M. Masticot, in accents more dismal than

Monsieur Grosgoulu," cried out Mdlle. Mimi
)ulette, from her end of the room, "before we

begin, I give you fair warning that I won't have any more of my costumes from the *costumier* of this theatre. I insist upon having my dresses sketched by Paul Créqui of the *Charivari*, and made by Worth. If you don't consent, I won't play the Queen of Egypt."

"And look here, Monsieur Grosgoulu!" exclaimed Mdlle. Sophie Mirabelle. "I've told you twice already, that I will not put up with only two dresses in a three-act piece. At the *Bouffes* they change their dresses each act. I wish you'd remember, too, that I've told the boot-maker twenty times at least to put gold heels and tassels to my dancing-boots and that he always forgets. Yesterday he sent me home three pairs of white satin boots with red heels and silk laces; but I won't have them. I shall send them back, and if he can't alter them, I must have new ones."

"I've something to say, too, Monsieur Grosgoulu," cried out Mdlle. Zephirine. "That champagne which you had served us yesterday, in the drinking-scene of *Le Roi Potiron*, wasn't *Cliquot;* and you know very well I never drink *Moët*. If it happens again, I shall cry out on the stage, 'This is gooseberry,' which will make the public laugh, and serve you right."

"Is there any sugar in the basin?" roared out

the deep voice of M. Ballon, the *basso-profondo*. "If so, be kind enough, somebody, to pass me a glass of *eau-sucrée:* this is like an oven!"

"Yes, true. Ugh, how hot it is!" assented the stage-manager. "You shall have all that you want, ladies," he added, placidly; "but I think you're wrong, Mdlle. Mimi, about Paul Créqui—he doesn't draw half so well as our artist."

"Yes, he does," said Mdlle. Mimi. "He's the only artist who knows my figure. Monsieur Javelin, what are you laughing at?"

"Honi soit qui mal y pense," answered M. Javelin, demurely. "I think Paul Créqui is a lucky artist."

During this interchange of apostrophes, M. Masticot had gone to a cupboard and drawn out a manuscript, which he laid upon the table. "This is *Le Bœuf à l'Huile,*" he remarked, with heart-rending melancholy. "If you are quite ready, gentlemen, we shall be happy to hear you."

"What's—a—going—a—to take place?" asked Count de José, adjusting his eyeglass in his left eye.

"Yes—a—same question as I was going to ask —a—myself," remarked Count de Nosé, performing the same service towards his dexter optic.

"Have you ever read a play before?" inquired

M. Javelin. "I suppose not. Ahem! I remember the first play I read myself—a deuced bad title; but it was twenty years ago, before I knew Langouste. I say, Langouste, come here and give our young novices a hint. Very valuable the hints of Langouste. Knows better than any man in the profession what trick to catch the public with. Make a stuffed bird laugh, Langouste would. By the way, which of you two is it that's going to begin?"

"You do the reading," said Trémolin; "you understand it better."

"No," said I, "I think you do."

"Let us draw lots then," suggested Théodore, recurring to his favourite method; and we drew as we had done the night before, but this time the task fell to him.

Counts de José and de Nosé, observing that nobody had answered their previous questions, here thought the time had come for standing up and making a statement.

"I—a—never heard—a—play read—a—before," began Count de José.

"Nor I—a," added Count de Nosé.

"You hold your tongues," exclaimed Mdlle. Triboulette, authoritatively. "Sit down yonder, both of you, and mind your behaviour. You, M. de José,

9*

take Bichon on your lap, and see you don't let him fall. Sophie, I wish you wouldn't blow tobacco-smoke into that pet's face, and make him sneeze."

"What is the name of the young man who is going to read?" asked Mdlle. Zephirine of the great Langouste, who was reclining in an armchair, paring his nails.

"Lémolins, Trémolins, or something of the kind," replied the great Langouste.

"Il n'est pas mal, ce jeune homme," rejoined Mdlle. Zephirine. "Il a une tête sympathique."

"Let us hear what his play is like," answered M. Langouste, curtly; and he shut up his penknife with a snap.

But this time the "jeune homme" with the "tête sympathique" had sat down at the table and opened his manuscript. "Silence, if you please, ladies," cried M. Grosgoulu. Théodore coloured slightly, and ran his fingers through his hair to give himself a countenance. Everybody was looking at him, and there was a general hush.

"*Ptolomée XXIII.*, *ou le Bœuf à l'Huile*," he began abruptly, giving out the title; then, gathering courage as he raised his voice, he proceeded to read the three acts.

IV.

I hope you will sympathize with the position of a writer who is obliged to state that a play in which he had a part was received with peals of laughter, cries of "Bravo!" and other encouraging demonstrations. But the fact is, that whatever may have existed in the joint composition of Trémolin and me, was certainly due to my colleague's wit, and not to mine; and under the circumstances, I am not quite sure that I have any right to be modest. I have been told of a plumber and glazier who, hearing somebody praise the architectural beauties of a new-built house in which he had just been putting a few panes of glass, blushed discreetly, and said, "Oh, sir, don't mention it." I am somewhat in the position of this plumber. I did little more than put a few panes of glass and do a little decorating to the house that Trémolin built, and if, on the strength of this, I were to take to blushing and playing modest, I am afraid the plumber and I would be rowing in the same boat. Let me speak unreservedly, then, and give Trémolin his due. To begin with, he read admirably, and before he had got to the end of the second page, had forced even the great Langouste to look up and smile. He was decidedly a man of parts, was this Langouste. On the bridge of his nose he wore a double eyeglass, which he took off and on as excitement grew upon him, and with which he beat time in the air when any passage was particularly to his liking. Monsieur Javelin, his friend, comported himself similarly; and the two exchanged telegraphic signals, which M. Grosgoulou, the stage-manager, watched with mute interest, and translated into language for the benefit of M. Masticot. The latter, according to his wont, remained utterly dejected and desponding; but a few excruciating groans which he uttered now and then testified that his attention was alive, and that he, too, was as near being amused as he could be.

I shall perhaps do well to give you some idea of the *Bœuf à l'Huile*, by making a short summary of the three Acts:—

ACT I.

Ptolemy XXIII , having obtained the throne of Egypt by the forcible ejection of Oleos XXVII., bethinks him of consolidating his dynasty by making friends with the favourite divinity of the Egyptians, the Ox Apis (le Bœuf à l'Huile, so called, because it was the duty of Raga-Muffin, the high-priest, and his twenty-four acolytes, to anoint his head and his tail every morning with macassar-oil, paid for out of the public taxes). But Raga-Muffin, who is in the confidence of the Ox, assures the King that Apis must decline to hold any terms with him unless he, Raga-Muffin, is immediately appointed Prime Minister, and is allowed to find posts of emolument for the twenty-four acolytes his kinsmen. The Ox, moreover, declares that his allowance of oil must be doubled, and paid for in specie instead of in kind, as heretofore. Should these conditions not be complied with he will make himself unpleasant to Ptolemy, and cause him to be turned off the throne within a certain specified time. The King, incensed at this language, snaps his thumb against the second finger of his right hand, and the curtain draws up at the precise moment when he is recommending Raga-Muffin to go on a trip to the city of Jericho, in the fertile land of the Jebusites. This recommendation is warmly backed up by, Proboscismos, the Prime Minister, and the high-priest is assisted in his exit from the royal palace by the personal vigour of this functionary, who then returns and proposes to Ptolemy that Raga-Muffin should be deprived of his office, and that a nephew of his—Proboscismos's—should be set up in his stead. But at this juncture there arrives in Egypt one Valkyrius-Gammo, a soothsayer of Latium, who suggests a third solution, which has the merit of being at once new and economical. He has observed that the oxen in his country eat much less wheaten bread and require much less oil for their tails than Apis seems to do. He thinks that if he were appointed high-priest, and were suffered to turn the four-and-twenty acolytes out of doors; he would do with half the present allowance of oil, and make Apis tractable and friendly into the bargain At this assurance a smile flits over the dark brow of Ptolemy, and he draws Valkyrius into an embrasure to ask him what he proposes to do with the surplus fund of the oil-money. Valkyrius answers that in his country, when there is a surplus in the budget, a time-honoured usage demands that it shall go into the pockets of the King, and he even points out that it would be no bad plan to ask the Wittenagemotal (or Egyptian assembly of legislators) for an additional grant of oil-money, which should, of course, find its way into the same sure haven as the surplus. Affected to tears by these soothing suggestions, Ptolemy clasps Valkyrius to his breast, and orders Proboscismos, whose countenance has been gradually lengthening during the discussion, to draw up letters patent under the great seal, and to have Valkyrius-Gammo proclaimed high-priest from one end of Egypt to the other. In despair at this order, the Prime Minister hurries off to the Queen, and describes Valkyrius as an unscrupulous individual, whose object it is to better himself at the expense of the land of Egypt, and to make his daughter Vanilla queen, after persuading Ptolemy to divorce his present spouse. To this the Queen Irubis replies stoutly that divorce is not lawful by the Code of Egypt, and that she does not care a fig for Gammo; but Proboscismos, who has a profound experience of legislative assemblies, explains the working of the Egyptian constitution, which is based on the equipoise and mutual-understanding system. When the King wishes anything, the Prime Minister is expected to wish it, and it is the duty of the Wittenagemotal to be of the same opinion. Thus, should Ptolemy desire a divorce, Proboscismos will be compelled to introduce a divorce-bill, which the legislators will immediately pass to prove their loyalty. Irubis does not wait to hear more; she catches up her golden distaff, and hastens off to have a little personal explanation with her lord. The last scene represents the banquetting-hall of the Ptolemies. Valkyrius-Gammo, in a brand-new gown, is sitting on the right of the King, who is pouring champagne into the goblet of Vanilla, the soothsayer's daughter. The Queen makes her unexpected entry at the moment when the tables are being cleared for a little choregraphic exercise, and the curtain falls upon a galop-infernal, danced by Ptolemy the King, Proboscismos the Prime Minister, Valkyrius-Gammo the soothsayer, Irubis the Queen, Vanilla the blue-eyed maiden, and the four-and-twenty acolytes, who have brought a *mandamus* from Raga-Muffin, condemning the King to excommunication.

ACT II.

The second Act opens to slow music. Irubis and Proboscismos have made common cause with the unfrocked Raga-Muffin, and a fell conspiracy is being organized by the three, with a view to removing Ptolemy from the throne, and setting up in his stead Amulis, son of Oleos, the deposed king. Irubis has long had a *tendre penchant* for Amulis, who on the deposition of his sire adopted the costume and habits of a boatman of the Nile, and was wont to come by moonlight under her Majesty's windows and play soft tunes on a Pandæan pipe. Before joining in the conspiracy, however, the Queen has taken care to have another conversation with the Prime Minister on the subject of the Egyptian constitution. Her object has been to ascertain whether, in the event of the conspiracy succeeding, it would be as easy for her to obtain a divorce from Ptolemy, as it would be, under existing circumstances, for Ptolemy to obtain a divorce from her. Proboscismos has appeased her fears. The Wittenagemotal, as he has explained, is an intelligent assembly, devoid of prejudices. So long as a sovereign is victorious and successful it asks no questions of him (or her), and it is only when he (or she) has come to grief that it ever ventures to be critical. "As for myself, madam," the statesman has added, "you can confide in me to the utmost. The eleven monarchs whom I have had the pleasure of serving could all testify to my honour that I invariably remained faithful to them until the hour when they were deposed."

The conspirators have accordingly met together in a lonely spot—in fact, on one of the Pyramids. Raga-Muffin has forgiven Proboscismos for his display of zeal in, kicking him downstairs, and Proboscismos has consented to forget that Raga-Muffin ever aspired to replace him as Prime

Minister. At the suggestion of Amulis, a proclamation is drawn up to assure the Egyptian people that the conspirators are only actuated by motives of the purest philanthropy; that what they pre-eminently desire is to see the Egyptians happy and free; that Ptolemy XXIII. is a tyrant; but that when Amulis ascends the throne every Egyptian shall have two loaves of bread *per diem*, and more money than he can spend. Proboscismos copies this proclamation on a model which has served eleven times already on similar occasions, and which he warrants to serve as many times more as necessity shall require. After this the conspirators concert their plan of action, and agree that the first use they will make of their victory will be to hang Valkyrius Gammo, and to shut up his daughter Vanilla in a wicker-work cage, which Irubis has with wise forethought ordered of a basket-maker in Memphis for the purpose. The scene concludes with an insurrection of the boatmen of the Nile at the call of Amulis, and a general *cancan* and breakdown by the rebels at the foot of the Pyramid. The four-and-twenty acolytes out of work take part in this dance as before, and at the termination of the performance an insurrectionary fleet rows off by moonlight up the Nile for Memphis; Irubis the Queen leading in a boat manned by sixteen oarsmen, of whom the handsome Amulis is the "stroke."

Meanwhile, however, Valkyrius-Gammo, the new custodian of the *Bœuf à l'Huile*, has got wind that there is mischief brewing against him, and is trying to make himself popular both with Ptolemy the King and Ptolemy's subjects. Unfortunately, he is not altogether so successful as he could desire. Ptolemy XXIII. seems preoccupied, and has been seen repeatedly to sit in a brown study for hours together, without attending to his royal duties or so much as condescending to wash his royal face. Even the bright eyes of Vanilla fail to arouse him. Upon being repeatedly pressed by Valkyrius, he at last ends by acknowledging that he has a big sorrow on his heart. On the day when Raga-Muffin was peremptorily dismissed from his functions as high-priest, the Ox Apis gave forth an alarming oracle, which has made his Majesty unquiet and miserable ever since. The gist of the oracle was this: that at no distant date Ptolemy XXIII. would be succeeded by a sovereign whose name began with an A and ended with an S. Upon hearing this Valkyrius-Gammo smiles, and prays his King to be of good cheer, pointing out that the oracle has a very simple interpretation. By the letters A and S the Ox can only mean that the sovereign who will succeed Ptolemy will be surnamed Asinus, but that, as this is no new thing in Egypt, there is not the slightest occasion for anxiety. At these words the King regains his spirits', for Valkyrius explains that Asinus is a Latin substantive, signifying a being of patient, gentle, laborious spirit; and he goes on to show that, if this Majesty likes to render the oracle harmless, all he has to do is to tack the epithet on to his own name, and so bring it actually to pass that Asinus has succeeded to Ptolemy. Of course the King adopts the suggestion with pleasure, and has himself proclaimed anew forthwith by the name of Ptolemy-Asinus. Valkyrius feels relieved; but new troubles instantly spring up for him in the shape of fifteen deputations who wait upon the King to remonstrate against the way in which the Ox Apis is being maltreated, starved, and neglected by its new pontiff. "Formerly," remark the memorialists (all respectable householders of Memphis), "the cities of Thebes and Memphis each voted 150 loaves of wheaten bread a day for the Ox; at present they are only asked for seventy-five,—a clear proof that the unfortunate divinity has not enough to eat. Furthermore, under the last high-priest, and from time out of mind previously, five-and-thirty gallons of refined oil had been devoted every day to the Ox's tail; whilst, under the new dispensation, half-a-pint of an inferior liquid is the most that has ever been reserved in a single day for the same venerated object." These facts are notorious. A baker and an oilman—the spokesmen of the deputations—comment upon them indignantly; the former remarking that ancient traditions must not lightly be laid aside, and the latter observing that religion, law, morality, order, and all that men hold most sacred, are gradually being swept away by a flood of new and infidel doctrines. Hereupon a warm scene ensues. Ptolemy XXIII., in language which the baker declares to be unparliamentary, requests the fifteen deputations to hurry out of his sight. The oilman is the first to withdraw, impelled by a signal from the King's foot. The others follow him; but Valkyrius-Gammo, who is standing near the door, gets unexpectedly caught up in the rush, and carried out yelling. The concluding scene of the second Act represents the great square of Memphis, and the fifteen deputations of Egyptians bearing Valkyrius, still screaming and resisting, towards the Temple of Apis. The baker and the oilman have each got hold of him by an ear; and the crowd are demanding with furious shouts to have the Ox brought out, in order that everybody may judge whether he is leaner now than he was a few months ago. The guards of Ptolemy-Asinus make a valiant attempt to rescue Valkyrius; and his daughter Vanilla throws herself on her knees before the baker, but all to no purpose. The fifteen deputations, suddenly swelled in magnitude by the arrival of the insurrectionary boatmen and the twenty-four acolytes, under the command of Raga-Muffin and Amulis, surge, howling and victorious, up the steps of the temple, set Gammo upon his legs, and insist upon his opening the door. Sardonic glances are exchanged at this juncture between Amulis, Proboscismos, Raga-Muffin, and the twenty-four acolytes. Valkyrius-Gammo, panting, turns the key in the lock and runs into the temple. A minute passes, and then a fearful cry is heard. Valkyrius, haggard and with his hair on end, rushes out upon the threshold with something in his hand. THE OX APIS IS GONE, AND THERE IS NOTHING LEFT OF HIM BUT THE SKIN!

ACT III.

At the commencement of the third Act, Valkyrius-Gammo, become white and lean from emotion, is thanking Ptolemy-Asinus for having'delivered him just in the nick of time from the fury of his enemies. Ptolemy had, in fact, appeared just at the precise moment, when Raga-Muffin, Amulis, and the parliamentary baker were taking sudden but unmistakable measures for despatching Gammo into a better world. It transpires, in the course of conversation, that Raga-Muffin himself and his acolytes have been arrested and thrown into prison. They were seized in the crowd dis-- guised as boatmen, and this'fact points clearly to the suspicion that it was they who stole the Ox in order to heap shame and misery upon their rival. Proboscismos, who arrives during the dialogue, endorses this view of the' case. Pending the result of the scrimmage between the royal troops and the insurgents, this prudent Minister retired to a secluded spot to watch the course of events. Now, however, that fortune has declared itself for the King, he sees no use in being a conspirator any longer, and so hastens to make friends with Valkyrius-Gammo, and to suggest that Raga-Muffin and the acolytes should be hanged out of hand as foul knaves and traitors. But the Queen Irubis, erewhile so incensed against her lord, has cooled considerably in her revolutionary zeal during the last four-and-twenty hours. In the first place the conspirators have been defeated ignominiously, and—what is much more humiliating—she has discovered beyond doubt, that the handsome Amulis had never for a moment contemplated marrying her in the event of the rebellion succeeding. Amulis is deeply in love with some one else. He loves a maiden with eyes like sapphires; and it was for the behoof of this damsel, and not for her Majesty's, that he had been in the habit of playing the Pandæan pipes after dark near the palace windows. Stung in her woman's vanity, Irubis vows revenge upon the giddy youth, and, in the meanwhile, deems it politic to conclude a treaty with Valkyrius-Gammo—she engaging not to conspire any more against that personage, if he, on his side, will promise to give up his scheme for marrying Vanilla with Ptolemy-Asinus. Valkyrius renounces this scheme with the greater readiness, as he had never for a moment entertained it; the supposed divorce having been all along a mere gratuitous supposition on the part of Proboscismos. "*Quelles drôles d'idées ont ces femmes!*" he soliloquizes in a stage aside. *"C'était pourtant là un fameux arrangement si j'y avais pensé plus tôt. Mais, voilà, les bonnes inspirations nous viennent toujours trop tard!"* Irubis reconciled with the King (who, indeed, had never suspected her of any share in the conspiracy) now obtains from him a search-warrant, which is confided to Belphegor, the captain of the King's guard, with orders to turn every house in Memphis upside down, and bring Amulis to punishment. The scene terminates with a lively chorus, expressive of mutual understanding, and a *pas de-quatre* by Ptolemy-Asinus, Proboscismos, Valkyrius-Gammo, and her Majesty. The luckless Amulis, during this time, has felt that pursuers were after him, and has found a refuge in the house of his beloved, the young lady with the sapphire eyes. Strange to say, he does not know the name of this charmer, having never seen her elsewhere than at her windows, in her dwelling near the palace. Accordingly, whilst he is being conducted by the young lady to her father's stable, where she intends concealing him in the corn-bin, he ventures upon the tender question,—*"Comment te nommes-tu?"* and is taken breathless upon hearing the reply,—*"Je m'appelle Vanilla."* However, it is too late to retreat, for, just as the lid of the corn-bin is being shut down, Valkyrius-Gammo, the father of Vanilla, returns to dinner: and almost immediately afterwards, Belphegor, the captain of the King's guard, in accordance with his instructions to leave no house unvisited, puts in an appearance with his search-warrant, and proceeds to examine the stables. Vanilla, in despair, sees no way out of the difficulty but by confessing to her father that she is in love with a gentleman—name unknown—whom it seems the police are looking after, and who is hiding at that moment in the corn-bin. Valkyrius, before consenting to a marriage, requests to know further particulars; and it is then that the fugitive, raising the lid of the corn-bin, proclaims himself as Amulis, and offers to become a loyal subject provided he is presented with a high post under Government, and suffered to marry Vanilla. As, after all, Amulis is the son of an ex-king, and the nearest heir to the throne in the event of the sudden decease of Ptolemy (life is very uncertain in Egypt), Valkyrius-Gammo perceives the advantages of the connection, and agrees to the union, if only the Queen will consent to it—which she does without much hesitation, being only too glad to get her supposed rival Vanilla out of the way. Thus, all seems on the point of ending well, and nothing more is required in the interests of poetic justice but to hang Raga-Muffin and the four-and-twenty acolytes. But Valkyrius-Gammo, who is in a forgiving mood, suggests to Ptolemy-Asinus that Raga-Muffin should be pardoned, on condition of his acknowledging what he has done with the Ox Apis. The ex-pontiff, thus questioned, ends by avowing that he and his kinsmen have killed the Ox and eaten him dressed "*à l'huile.*" But he adds, in extenuation, that this is not the first time, for that he had always been in the habit of killing the different oxen under his charge as soon as they got fat, and that the people of Egypt have worshipped, at the smallest reckoning, some threescore of Apises in the course of five years. This confession is deemed so entertaining, that Raga-Muffin is at once let loose, and there and then sets off to found a restaurant, with the signboard "*Au Bœuf à l'Huile;*" promising, as he goes, that any of the nobility and gentry of Memphis who honour him with their patronage shall have a taste of his delicacy, and smack their lips at it. The last scene again represents the great square of Memphis and the marriage of Amulis and Vanilla, together with the procession of the Ox Apis. For, of course, by this time, a new Ox has been procured (a prize-ox twice as fat as the last), and the people of Egypt have been made happy by the assurance that in order to make certain that the Ox shall never become thin, the public will be taxed double that year to pay for oil; and that every baker in Thebes and Memphis shall, moreover, have the privilege of providing the Ox with two loaves of the best wheaten bread each morning, gratis. Naturally the wedding-breakfast of Amulis and Vanilla takes place at the newly established restaurant, "*Le Bœuf à l'Huile,*" where the four-and-twenty acolytes, shaved and washed and transformed into waiters, officiate with civility and decorum.

When Théodore Trémolin closed his manuscript at the conclusion of the third Act, there was a treble salvo of applause, and the whole of the audience, rising like one man, clustered round to offer their congratulations. Théodore, athirst, wiped his brow and poured himself out a glass of water, seeming to understand less than anybody what there was to be so enthusiastic about, and appearing rather mystified than otherwise at the compliments.

"It's capital!" cried Mdlle. Triboulette. "I'll be the Queen Irubis: but there are one or two passages you'll have to lengthen for me; you've not given me enough of dialogue. Monsieur Grosgoulu, mind you write to Paul Créqui this week, and send him a copy of the play. He must sketch the dresses for me immediately."

"I'll play Vanilla," exclaimed Mdlle. Zephirine; "but you must make me come on more often than you do, Monsieur Semolina. I should like to be in that scene of the boats on the Nile, and you must tell M. Grosgoulu that I shall want at least four changes of dress."

M. Emile Javelin was clapping Trémolin on the back.

"They pay ten per cent. author's profits* in this house," he remarked. "If your piece runs a hundred nights, your fortune's begun. But if I were you, I would make a little alteration in the first act—it's too long."

There was some whispered consultation between the stage-manager and the melancholy lessee, M. Masticot; after which the latter, turning to us with a bow, into which he infused as much courtesy and

---

* It is not the custom in France to pay a lump sum for a play, as is often done in England. The author receives so much per cent. of the gross receipts according to the number of Acts in his piece. Some theatres pay as high as twelve per cent.; and I may remark that in the case of extravaganzas this is not always fair to the managers. A good many extravaganzas depend entirely for their success upon the scene-painter and costumier; and it is rather hard, under the circumstances, for the authors to take the lion's-share of profits to themselves.

lugubriousness as was humanly possible, said, "Gentlemen, we accept your play on the usual terms, subject to the permission of the Censors. I will have it sent to the Censorship this very night."

"Ah, yes, the Censors, I had forgotten them!" exclaimed M. Javelin, putting his tongue suddenly in his cheek and becoming pensive.

A sort of grim chuckle answered his observation, and to the speechless consternation of Trémolin and me, the following words fell from the lips of the great Langouste, like so many drops of freezing water in our midst—"I advise you two young gentlemen not to be too hopeful, for your play will be prohibited. I warn you beforehand."

I remembered now that the great Langouste, though he had appeared amused at several of the passages, had never once clapped his hands or cried, "Bravo!" Trémolin and I looked at him horror-stricken.

"Prohibited!" I faltered, with a lump in my throat. "Who by?"

"By M. Buche," said the great Langouste.

"But who is M. Buche? What is he?"

This simple question appeared to take the great Langouste by surprise. He stared at me, and arched his eyebrows: "Ah," said he, "you don't know M. Buche!" and he grinned horribly.

V.

I leave you to judge of the state of mind in which Théodore Trémolin and I walked home. To see before one a cup filled with some bright red tempting wine, and to be told at the moment of raising it to one's lips that a mysterious individual, never heard of or seen before, was waiting to dash it from one's mouth? Who was M. Buche? what was he? where was his lair? what sort of a heart had he? was there any chance of propitiating him? All these were questions which we asked ourselves as we trudged along, and I verily believe that if we had been anywhere else than on the crowded Boulevards, we should both of us have sat down and cried. You see, we were neither of us senators nor academicians, as M. Buche was, and what might be capital sport to him was likely to prove very poor fun to us. We saw "Buche" figured in letters of fire over the door of every official-looking house, and on the forehead of every official-looking individual we met. Poor Trémolin was civil and humble to a sergent-de-ville who trod on his toe. After all, was not a policeman a twig of the great administrative tree of which M. Buche was one of the big branches; and had we not every interest to be abject and down-on-all-fours before every personage of any degree who had any ramifications whatever with that dreaded Administration? Perhaps it was fortunate for the dignity of human nature that we did not meet the Emperor's carriage out that afternoon. In our then temper of mind we should assuredly have salaamed ignobly, and held ourselves up as objects of derision to the public.

I am sure I cannot tell you how we passed that night, nor the day following, nor the night after that. I have uncertain recollections of a visit to the Hebrew who had hired us our clothes, and of another visit by night to an edifice with a flag over the door, to obtain the wherewith to pay him. I think we spent our day looking out of the window and counting the number of sparrows who came and perched during a given time on the roof opposite. There was no necessity for talking in this pastime. It allowed us to sit by each other and pursue our own thoughts quietly and unobtrusively. I have kept the recollection of one sparrow, who came several times, and appeared to look at me wistfully, as if he wanted to say something. Perhaps he was astonished at our miserable looks.

We had begged Emile Javelin that he would kindly write and tell us what was the decision of the Censorship, and he had promised to do so. His letter came on the third day by the earliest post, whilst half Paris was still in bed. The sun was fill-ing our garret with a clear, bright, gay yellow light, which would have made a paradise of it, had we been happy and hopeful, as Béranger probably was when he wrote—

"Dans un grenier qu'on est bien à vingt ans."

This time there was no hesitation about breaking the seal of the envelope; we burst it open at once, silently, half-savagely. This is what we read:—

"My Dear M. Marmelot,—I am sorry to say that Langouste guessed right—he always does guess right does Langouste. The Censors, M. Buche at their head, have refused to license your play. However, per-haps all is not lost, for I have prevailed upon one of the committee, whom I know slightly, to give the *"Bœuf à l'Huile"* a second reading at eleven o'clock to-morrow in your presence. M. Buche will be there—*absit omen!*—and if you try hard you may be able to induce him to pass the play with some altering.

"Cordially and sympathizingly,
"Emile Javelin."

"To-morrow, at eleven," repeated Trémolin. "That means in three hours, for the note was written yesterday." And he began searching his pockets for the sum of small coin necessary to obtain a new loan of the Hebrew's clothes. All he could muster, however, was seven sous, and another visit to the edi-fice with the flag over the door became necessary. We parted that morning with our last remnant of 'books, and with a fiddle of Trémolin's; but at eleven we were both be-coated and be-hatted according to the fashions then prevailing, and we passed the sentry at the door of the Ministerial office, where the Censorship sat, without being taken for two professional beggars, as many dramatists, in the same predicament as we, have been before us.

What trim-looking, courteous places those Ministerial offices are! Although it was spring, and nobody in the streets felt cold, there were warm and glowing fires in all the lobbies and passages. An usher with a silver chain round his neck asked us deferentially whom we desired to see. "Dramatic Censorship, gentlemen?" he repeated, after us. "Third door on the right, second landing. M. Buche has just arrived, I believe." And he bowed as if we were two ambassadors. "Dramatic Censorship," echoed somebody further on; and perhaps this one took us for M. Sardou and M. Dumas the younger, for he added, parenthetically, "We are accustomed to see a great many of your profession, gentlemen; some very poor ones, though, among them." And he gave himself a pinch of snuff, as if to dispel the contamination of these poor ones. In the antechamber of the Censors we found still more politeness. "MM. Trémolin and Marmelot, I believe?" asked a well-dressed young clerk, consulting a paper.

"This way, if you please, gentlemen." And, with a smirk, he threw open the door of a room, in which six gentlemen, all more or less bald, were gathered in a circle round the fireplace. We were standing in the presence of the Censors.

The centre of the group was a towering man in a bun-brown coat, and with three rolls of white neck-cloth round his throat. In one of his button-holes was a scarlet rosette, and he wore shoes over which his socks could be seen. He had apparently break-fasted well, for he was rubicund and happy, and tossed a massive bunch of gold seals that were fastened to his watch-chain with a great deal of good-humour and complacency. A glance sufficed to show that he was the great planet, and that the others round him were mere satellites. At the moment of our coming in he had been cracking a joke, and the five bald gentlemen around him were laughing in unison, each with the same expression on his face.

When our names were announced the laughing abated, and M. Buche—for we both guessed that the man in the brown coat must be he — M. Buche coughed and dived both hands into his hind-pockets. This was all the good-morning he gave us; but he went and took his seat at the round table, whither his five coadjutors followed him, and began forthwith beating tattoos on the cloth with their paper-knives.

"How is your rheumatism this morning, M. Rouscot?" asked one Censor of another in a whisper of condolence.

"Thank you, it let me sleep last night," answered the other, with a nod.

"There's a great deal of rheumatism about at the present moment," remarked a third Censor.

"Have you ever tried camphor lotions, Rouscot?" interposed M. Buche, in a tone of benevolent interest. "I always use them myself, and find them very serviceable."

During this time the least bald of the company had been ferreting about amongst a heap of papers, from which he ultimately drew a manuscript which we recognized as ours. As he turned over the leaves, we could see that it was literally slashed with red pencil marks. The Censor assured himself that he had got hold of the play he wanted and handed it respectfully to M. Buche.

. . I assure you it would have been worth paying twenty francs to watch the features of this great Senator and Academician as he took our manuscript in his hand and surveyed the title. There was a look of cool disdain, such as no language could paint, and a shrug of the shoulders, which placed us

and our works low—so low in the category of
humanity, that the five satellite Censors shuddered
and gazed upon us as the jury do at a convict when
the verdict is guilty, and the judge is deliberating
as to whether it shall be fifteen or twenty years'
penal servitude. M. Buche lurched and whispered
something in the ear of the Censor on his right.
We were just able to catch the words "Inexpressibly
vulgar titles," "prostitution of dramatic art," "de-
secration of antiquity," "low standard of modern
literature." M. Buche then faced us and said neither
angrily nor rudely, but with calm majesty—

"MM. Trémolin and Marmelot, you have asked
for a second reading of this—this"—(M. Buche hesitated; he could not bring himself to say "play")
—"of this—composition, and the examining committee are ready to accede to your request. But I
think it as well to forewarn you that no amount of
reading can alter our irrevocable determination,
which is to prohibit the performance of your work.
I beg your pardon, what did you say?"

"I was only saying," remarked Trémolin, "that
under the circumstances a new reading was perhaps
superfluous."

"Exactly so," assented M. Buche. "We here
round this table have a duty to perform—a duty, I

may say a sacred duty, towards Society. In the discharge of our functions we endeavour to show as much indulgence as we may with safety; indeed, I may say that this indulgence is, in our case, not a choice but a necessity. I have no wish, gentlemen, to wound your—your—susceptibilities: but you must be as well aware as I that the standard of modern literature is lower than it ever has been in the world's history, save, perhaps, at that barbarous period when Pharamond and his Franks destroyed the civilization of the Romans in Gaul and transformed this country into a wilderness. If, therefore, we were not to temper justice with indulgence—with the most extreme indulgence—we could pass no play—no, not one; for all are bad alike: it is only a question of degrees. However, there are certain limits at which our indulgence must stop. *Est modus in rebus*, as Flaccus has pertinently said. Society has wisely set up certain barriers which are called morality and order. When we see a tendency—nay, an overt intention—to transgress these barriers, it is our mission to interpose, as we distinctly do in the present instance; refusing to license a composition in which the throne and the altar are turned into ridicule, and the principle of legislative assemblies is covered with much unmerited odium."

A murmur of approval from the five satellites

testified to the cordial echo which these sentiments found: M. Buche proceeded:—

"I know there is a marked propensity, in writers of the present period of literary decline, to sneer at all the institutions which have obtained the consecration of past ages. Neither religion nor the solid principles of executive government as represented by royalty are safe from aspersion. You have proved it too well in the present composition by making of your King Ptolemy a dullard, of your Queen Irubis a woman of unstable affections, and of your Prime Minister Probo—Probo—yes, Proboscismos (just heavens, what a medley of inanities!) a personage such—such—yes, such as I am proud to say has never been seen in this country."

"But we were talking of Egypt," submitted Trémolin, respectfully.

"Possibly, sir, in word, but not in spirit," replied Monsieur Buche sternly. "In such works as these, sir, the intention is everything. You aim at satire, sir; yes, at satire; and, I cannot refrain from saying it, at most improper and subversive satire. Do you think, sir, that we have not detected that by Ptolemy XXIII.—mark that perfidious III.—you intend to designate our present sovereign; by Proboscismos, his Excellency the Prime Minister; by Amulis the pretender, the Duc d'Aumale; by Raga-

Muffin—Raga-Muffin, gentlemen" (this to his fellow-Censors), "is a word of Anglo-Saxon origin signifying *vaurien*, *va-nus-pieds*—by Raga-Muffin, I say, a distinguished contemporary prelate universally revered for his saintly qualities; and by Valkyrius-Gammo" (here M. Buche turned scarlet)—"yes, by Valkyrius-Gammo, the ridiculous sage, probably *MYSELF!*"

This was a thunder-clap. Trémolin leaned against me for support: "Oh, mon Dieu!" he said, and fell upon a chair, shaking with interminable laughter.

M. Buche stood bolt still, gazed at us with petrified dignity, and then walked solemnly towards the bell, which he pulled.

A messenger appeared.

"Show these gentlemen out," said M. Buche.

VII.

Half an hour afterwards we were walking back home along the Boulevards. We were possibly not in the best of spirits, but we were still laughing, and Trémolin had begun to talk almost unconcernedly of our misadventure. At the Rue St. Honoré there was a confusion of carriages which caused us to stop. A superb barouche, with a pair of prancing greys, was blocking up the street, and a crowd had gathered on the pavement to stare at the auburn-haired beauty in lilac silk, and the diminutive Havannah dog, who were the sole occupants of the vehicle. Of a sudden the lady in lilac silk leaned forward, and began to gesticulate with her parasol.

"M. Semolina! M. Marmalade!"

We recognized Mdlle. Mimi Triboulette. Behind her, at about twenty yards' distance, Counts de José and de Nosé, on horseback, were serving as escort. We raised our hats, and were going to pass on.

"No, no! one moment!" she cried; "not in such a hurry! Where do you come from, gentlemen?"

"From the Censorship," I said.

"*Eh, bien?*"

"Refused," answered Trémolin.

"*Oh, mon Dieu!*" exclaimed Mdlle. Mimi in dismay. "*Et moi qui avais déjà commandé mes robes. Vite, Alphonse, vite! Faites tourner les chevaux chez ma couturière!*"

And this was the epitaph of our first success.

UNE PÉTROLEUSE.

UNE PÉTROLEUSE.

A SOUVENIR OF VERSAILLES.

I.

Some hundred years ago a very great French lady, who had led a gallant life in her youth, bethought her of founding a prize for virtue in her old age. The locality she selected as the scene of her munificence was her own manorial village of Champterre; and in order that she might not be frustrated of the, to her, somewhat novel spectacle of virtue getting the best of it in this world's race, she determined to institute the prize during her lifetime, instead of bequeathing it to be wrangled for between her heirs and the legatees after her death, as is the more usual way. So a man of law was sent for, and drew up a deed of gift with conditions clearly set forth. Every year the "notables" of the village were to assemble on the 15th June, the feast of St. Modest, and decide between them who was the most virtuous girl in the village. If there were a debate on this delicate question, and

opinions stood pretty equally divided, the right of
giving the casting vote was to devolve on the oldest
of the "notables," who, by reason of his years, might
be presumed a shrewder connoisseur of the point at
issue than his compeers. You will have noticed,
by the way, that I say "notable," and not municipal
councillor, the fact being that municipal councillors
were then not yet invented. Those were the dark
ages of politics, when a farmer was stupid enough
to stick to farming, and a labourer to labouring,
without claiming the privilege to meddle with matters he didn't understand. I have even heard that
neither farming nor labouring were much the worse
on that account, but this I decline to believe. Once
the candidate chosen, with or without debate, she
was to be proclaimed maiden-queen of Champterre,
and on the next Sunday but one following her election to be conducted to the parish church and there
solemnly crowned with a chaplet of white roses, to
please herself, and presented with a dowry of five
hundred silver francs to please her future husband·
The proceedings were to conclude with a dinner
for the notables, and climbing a greasy pole, with
other appropriate amusements, for the rest of the
public.

Well, the annual ceremony proved a success. So
long as the great French lady lasted, she presided

over it in person, encouraging the prize-winners by many edifying examples, drawn from lives other than her own, to persevere on the path they had adopted, and assuring them that virtue led to every good thing in this life as well as out of it—which was amiable on her part, though superfluous, for the moment virtue led to five hundred silver francs its value was sufficiently understood and appreciated by even the meanest intellects at Champterre. By the end of a few years' time, not a damsel in the village but steadfastly resolved to be virtuous until the age of twenty—twenty being the limit when one ceased to be eligible for the francs; and in the whole country-side around, Champterre , acquired the enviable reputation of rearing incomparable vegetable-marrows—which it had done before the Prize—and no less incomparable maidens, which it had only begun to do afterwards. And so time. wore on. Gradually, however, as the world emerged from the dark ages already mentioned, and glided triumphantly into the present century of enlighten+ ment, certain changes took place. To begin with, the notables disappeared; they had never done anybody harm and so were not regretted. Then came nine municipal councillors, who pulled bunches out. of one another's hair in discussing the local rates,: howled at one another across a deal table in plan+

ning a local road, and were generally voted an improvement. Hitherto the yearly fête at Champterre had been a purely family concern, attended at most by the populations of surrounding villages: the municipal council hit upon the excellent idea of making it as public as possible. The desire to stimulate virtue had, of course, less to do with this than the wish to fill the municipal coffers, but in either case the results were likely to be the same. If crowds could be brought down from Paris, it was probable that money would be brought with them, and if money were brought, then might not only the municipal coffers be replenished, but the maiden-prize be increased, and virtue thus earn an accrued meed of recompense? So a cattle-show was added to the other attractions of the festival, then a fair, then fireworks, until little by little, and attraction by attraction, the crowning of the "Rosière," as it was called, became—railways aiding—one of the most popular sights within a hundred miles of Paris, and a thing which all strangers were expected to go and see, just like the Palace of the Tuileries, where sovereigns lived, and the Place de la Roquette, where criminals died. In proportion, however, as the importance of the spectacle itself was enhanced, so of a necessity was that of the Rosière. At first she had been a poor girl, receiving just her crown

of roses with her five hundred francs and no more;
but when strangers took to coming and dropping
offertories into the velvet bags that were handed
round to them during service, then the dower rose
to be much nearer five thousand francs than five
hundred, and became *de facto* worth possessing by
others than poor girls, daughters of cottage labourers
and such like. It is said that strange debates began
then to be heard in the municipal council. One
half of the council being at perpetual feud with the
other half, as it is natural, just, and proper that the
two halves of every council should be, the virtue-
elections were turned into occasions for yearly con-
tests in which sarcasm, invective, and scathing re-
criminations were exchanged with a freedom well
worthy of a wider field. The opposition half of the
council—small but deep-mouthed after the manner
of oppositions—would periodically and bitterly ac-
cuse the majority of seeking to foist upon the
public Rosières of dubious quality, whose sole claim
to election lay in their bright eyes, their ready
smiles, or in the fact that they were the daughters,
nieces, cousins, or what not of members of the
majority. To which the members of the majority
would indignantly retort that if the opposition had
their way, there would be none but Rosières who
squinted, were humpbacked, or went on crutches—.

and indeed it is a fact that, just as in larger national assemblies, oppositions seem to take a peculiar delight in proposing bills which they know to be unpassable, so at Champterre the opposition systematically and virulently patronized a set of candidates of whom the most that can be said is that their virtue must have cost them little, seeing that no human being would have been so devoid of taste as to assail it. I need scarcely add that in the upshot the majority always ended by carrying their point, and that the opposition, having no other means of protest, were reduced to the time-honoured expedient of circulating feeble jokes and covert innuendos damaging to the reputation of the Rosière. Whence it arose that, public opinion being generally on the side of the opposition—as the audiences at plays are in favour of the amusing actors—a whole host of jovial anecdotes obtained currency; notably one to the effect that, on a certain memorable occasion, a young lady had, by dint of favouritism, been elected Rosière who—who—— But, pardon me, I am afraid I was going to tattle.

Let me only repeat, then, that, after being in existence a good century, the Fête de la Rosière had come to be established as a national institution, and that one day in the year 186—, never having seen the sight, I readily consented to a proposal—

made overnight at the club by young Gaston de Floriant, my old school-friend—that a few of us should make up a party and go. Ah, how well I remember that Sunday!

It was one of those Parisian days that one drinks in, as it were, like·frothy champagne. Everybody seemed afoot. Fresh bonnets and summer dresses flashed by in yellow-wheeled flies, other bonnets and other dresses flitted over the pavements shading themselves with pink paràsols from the golden arrows which the sun was shooting, and escorted by white waistcoats, Panama hats, and those weightless alpaca coats which the Frenchman loves when the weather is hot. In the cafés the glasses jingled and the early coffee-cups mingled their aroma to those of the Boulevard cigars. *"Six, deux!"* and *"Double Six!"* cried out fanatical players of dominoes. *"Le Roi!"* echoed no less fanatical plays of écarté. "Qui a demandé *L'Indicateur des Chemins de Fer?"* sang out the headlong waiter. "Moâ!" responded the British tourist. "Circulez, Messieurs!" pleaded the white-gloved policeman. "Couronnement! Rosière! Champterre! Trains Express!" said the pink posters that papered the kiosks and walls. "Couron-nement de la Rosière! Billets d'aller et retour!" clamoured the saffron posters of a rival company. And so on we hurried, through street and over

crossing, elbowing and being elbowed, apologizing
and being apologized to, until we trooped into the
station, where a gay, tumultuous, beflowered multitude was choking up the waiting-rooms to the number of a thousand, two thousand, three thousand—
who knows?—for one might as well have tried to
count the dahlias at a prize-show, or the mocking-
birds in a tropical forest.   And what spirits and
what laughter!   A French holiday throng has always
vivacity enough and to spare; but everybody brings
his or her best of best moods to see the Rosière
crowned, this being, of all others, the fête most after
the French heart.   We had a stand of ten minutes,
during which well-known jokes, that pass current
once a year, resounded with the clink of coin in a
gold-room.   Ten minutes; and then of a sudden
back slid the doors of the waiting-rooms: nimbly to
one side jumped the attendant guards; and, like a
thirsty herd unpenned, away we scurried altogether
down the platform, racing for places.   The train was
stormed; parasols were dropped, many a noble um-
brella disappeared for ever in the scrimmage; and
ever and anon rose the cries: "Pardon, Madame."
"Oh, Monsieur, ma jupe!"   "Monsieur, we are already eleven in this compartment; indeed there isn't
room."   "Oh, mon Dieu, Messieurs, I have lost my
husband—I can't see him!"   "Soyez tranquille, Ma-

dame, un mari ça se retrouve; ce n'est pas comme une valeur quelconque." "Messieurs, have you seen my wife—a blue dress with a primrose bonnet?" "Certainly, Monsieur; just passed on the arm of a captain of dragoons." And so on, like the bubbling of rivers, until, the carriages being packed, the guards entered into wild conflicts with individuals who wanted to ride by standing on the steps, and clinging to the door handles sooner than not ride at all. When these were at length, to their unbounded indignation, precluded imperilling their necks, there was a moment's peace, and Gaston de Floriant, who was always dressed within an inch of his life, exclaimed, fanning himself with his handkerchief: "Well, this is the kind of thing I like; it's a Turkish bath before starting."

Our party was of twelve; but, for convenience' sake, we had paired away in couples, and I was mated with Floriant. In the same carriage with us were two others of our set: Cirobois (ycleped the Court Jester, because at the Tuileries soirées he was one of the few beings who possessed the faculty of making a certain august Personage smile), and Braungesicht of the Prussian Embassy. Braungesicht followed Cirobois everywhere like a tame bear, and was the unconscious butt of that gentleman's wit—Cirobois being one of those social scourges with a face like a Nuremberg nut-cracker, who never smiled, was of lugubrious demeanour, and experimented all his hoaxes upon poor Braungesicht, as *in animâ vili*, before trying them on the community. Had Cirobois been born with a wooden instead of a golden spoon in his mouth, he might have made the fortune of a comic paper or of a Boulevard play-house; but being rich with the accumulated millions of a defunct uncle in the wine-growing-and-adulterating-way (whom he regretted being unable to mourn, as he conscientiously expressed it), he was in a position to devote the whole of his talents to the mystification of the upper circles of society. Gaston de Floriant, I should mention, was a Marquis of the Rue de Lille—a patented Marquis, with trade-mark registered, as Cirobois put it. Twenty-seven years old, rich, singularly handsome, and *blasé*, he had quarrelled with the Faubourg St. Germain, because the dowagers of that noble quarter objected to his frequenting Bonapartist drawing-rooms; and he was not on particularly good terms with the Bonapartist drawing-rooms, because he was never to be caught in the nets of matrimony which the matrons of the Chaussée d'Antin so industriously set for him, his coronet, and his castle in Poitou. Add to this, that he fought on an average three duels a year, and that his adversaries were somehow always

married men, and you will have a picture of M. de
Floriant complete. The other seats in the carriage
were occupied by two men, one in a grey coat, the
other in a white; and by the presumable wives of
these passengers—the first young and attired in
lilac, the second less young and slightly rouged.

"What are we waiting for?" proceeded Floriant,
restoring his handkerchief to his pocket, and fasten-
ing the button of one of his fresh-butter-coloured
gloves.

"Yes. Vy are ve vaiting?" inquired Braungesicht, whose French by the way, was better than his
accent.

"It's the rule to wait," explained Cirobois, thrust-
ing his head out of the window. "Railways are
schools for patience, like marriage and the toothache.
But, hullo! *tstt! tstt!*" and he began waving one of
his hands. "It's Mirabelle, with a whole cargo of
white roses in tow."

And so it was: Mdlle. Mirabelle, the famous
flower-girl of a very famous sporting-club, was scud-
ding full sail down the platform, contemptuously
regardless of all functionaries who protested there
was no more room. Stout, Spanish-eyed, and attired in a fancy costume of blue and white, she carried slung in front of her a tray-basket full to over-
flowing with white roses. Behind her a servant in

livery groaned under the weight of two other such
baskets, likewise full, but closed to the public eye.
Mdlle. Mirabelle found flower-selling profitable
enough to keep liveried footmen and a brougham,
not to speak of diamond bracelets and other trifles.
Panting, she ran down·the whole length of the train,
looking for a vacant place, and distributing unem-
barrassed smiles as she ran. At our carriage she
stopped.

"M. de Floriant, M. Cirobois, a seat," she laughed.

"What on earth can you be going to do at Champterre?" asked Cirobois, amused. "You'll feel as
much in your element there as——"

"Never mind comparisons," interrupted Mdlle.
Mirabelle. "Have you a seat? No. Then take
some of my flowers." And becoming a little demure
as she caught sight of the ladies in the carriage, she
threw each of us four a wired rose, then lifted her
basket bodily in the carriage, and said, "Fleurissez-
vous, Mesdames, fleurissez-vous."

"For whom is this bouquet?" asked Floriant,
lifting a white nosegay a foot and half in dia-
meter.

"For you, Monsieur le Marquis; you ought to
buy it, and throw it to the Rosière. It's the custom,"
said she, dropping into her satchel the four napoleons
we had paid her—for, in dealing with acquaintances,

this young lady never gave change, which prevented mistakes. "See here what a noble one it is! but not too good. The Rosière's name is Félicie Lallouette; and just wait till you've seen her before you talk of beauty. Her father's a nurseryman who supplies me with flowers; and that's why I'm going down to-day."

"To set his daughter a good example," suggested Cirobois.

"No, to wish her joy," said Mdlle. Mirabelle, innocently. "You'll take the bouquet, Marquis?"

"You zay she is bretty?" asked Braungesicht, gravely.

"Divine, M. le Baron; and here is another bouquet, which you can throw—same price as the other, only five napoleons." And she held up a fellow-one to the first bouquet, bound with white satin ribbons and silver cord.

There were three like this. Floriant, who had not been able to help noticing (he never could help noticing these things) that the youngest of the two ladies with us looked extremely pretty in her lilac dress, took two of the bouquets, and with the perfect grace which a long career of gallantry had lent him, requested permission of the man in the white coat and the man in the grey to offer them to their respective wives. Which permission the two coats,

being already considerably abashed by the discovery
that they were travelling in the company of a live
marquis and baron, accorded amidst paroxysms of
hat-lifting and reddening acknowledgments that did
not fairly subside for the next five minutes. The
lilac dress blushed. Her companion would have
followed suit but for the rouge. As it was, she did
her best, naturally persuaded that the compliment
was wholly for her.

"And my third bouquet?" ejaculated Mdlle. Mirabelle, coaxingly.

"It's too cheap for me," responded Cirobois.
"Roses in July are scarce. I won't have you robbing
yourself."

Here the engine whistle sounded.

"Well, Marquis, I'll keep the bouquet for you,"
said Mdlle. Mirabelle, stepping back. "I shall be
down by the next train, and I am sure you'll ask
me for it before the day is over." And as the
wheels were turning she put a jewelled hand to her
lips, blew one of the ten thousand kisses she kept
in store for occasions like the present, and in
another moment became a white speck in the
distance.

"Dat is von fine girl!" ejaculated Braungesicht.

"And modest and retiring—sole support of four
aged grandmothers and as many grandfathers!" ex-

claimed Cirobois with feeling as we whirled out of the station.

"You don't say so!" remarked the grey coat, respectfully; "four grandmothers!"

"Yes; her father and mother both married twice, which accounts for it," proceeded Cirobois, quietly. "But have you never seen her?"

"I live in the Rue St. Denis—dealer in colonial produce, at your service," stammered the grey coat, delighted to see that Floriant was talking to his wife. "It's only on Sundays we manage to get out, only on Sundays—ahem!"

This last exclamation was caused by the lilac dress stamping furtively on his foot.

"Only on Sundays—that's like me when I sold baked potatoes on the top of the Colonne Vendôme," murmured Cirobois, who had noticed the foot-stamping. "Hot work for the fingers, Monsieur; but cool work for the head. I made my fortune by it."

"God bless my soul!" cried the man in the grey coat, while the lilac dress started and glanced with surprise at her husband's interlocutor.

"You were saying, then, that this year's Rosière is your daughter?" proceeded Cirobois, with imperturbable composure.

"Pardon me, I—I—never," stuttered the grey

coat, rather bewildered—"I think you mistake. We are only going down to see the sight. But I have a brother who is a municipal councillor at Champterre, and who helped to elect——"

"Ah, helped to elect! Yes, I was a municipal councillor myself once, and know what it is. You may tell your brother how much I sympathize with him, Monsieur," groaned Cirobois. "Twelve men exciting themselves in a close room, with no refreshment on the table but a tumbler of pump-water— that's a municipal council. And you say, then, that the Rosière—I beg your pardon, what were the interesting observations you let fall about the Rosière?"

"My husband must have said that Mdlle. Lallouette is the prettiest girl at Champterre," interposed the lilac dress, coming to her disconcerted spouse's rescue; "and if M. le Marquis be an admirer of beauty," added she, turning a little archly to Floriant, "he will find himself repaid for his journey."

"Oh, Madame," murmured Floriant, "you forget that after being dazzled by the flame of a wax-taper, no great impression can be produced upon one by a rushlight." Which was a skilful compliment, for had Floriant been a novice, he would have whispered that after beholding the sun, a man might with impunity face the moon, and not been understood; but the lilac dress, being wont to sell colonial produce (which is merely the French for grocery and candles), quickly seized the allusion to the difference between a five-and-twenty sou "four" and a farthing dip; and coloured with pleasure up to the roots of her pretty chestnut hair.

I think it was perhaps a lucky thing for the man in the grey coat that at this juncture the train stopped, and a porter with a rose in his button-hole (everybody seemed be-rosed that day) shouted out, "Champterre!"

II.

Certes it had been a proud day for Yves Lallouette, nurseryman and gardener, when M. Parbouillaud, Mayor of Champterre, followed by half his municipal council, had come to him and said, "Yves, your daughter is elected Rosière."

Had Yves been a sharp man he would have put two and two together, and remembered, firstly, that on the council was a certain Colin Grainereau, a farmer, with a pointed nose, his neighbour; secondly, that this farmer loved his, Yves's, daughter; and thirdly, that he had asked her in marriage and been accepted just one fortnight, day for day, before the election. But Yves was not a sharp man, and so drew no conclusions whatever from this assemblage of circumstances. When Mayor Parbouillaud made his statement, Yves accepted it as a bit of good fortune sent direct to him by Providence, and he figured the sign of the Cross three times, kissing his thumb at the end of that ceremony, which, as everybody knows, is a sure recipe for good luck. Then having made the half-council half-drunk with white wine, which he fished up with a rope from the well where he was accustomed to let it cool, he shook off his wooden shoes and crept up on tip-toe to apprise his daughter Félicie, who was ironing the kerchief she intended wearing at mass next Sunday, and not dreaming of anything in particular.

Félicie had no mother, brothers, or sisters. She lived alone with her father and an old aunt, who cooked for them; and, as a natural consequence, she did and said what she pleased, and Yves Lallouette was sure to find it good. It was undoubtedly a pity that this should have been so, for no flower in Yves's hot-house, no blossom in his choicest beds, could have borne comparison with Félicie—"My pet flower of all," as he would so often say. But like those plants that have been neither propped nor trimmed, and push their shoots in every direction, Félicie's nature had run wild. She was a young creature all impulse, with good qualities and

dangerous instincts so evenly balanced in her, that
it depended upon mere hair's-breadth chance which
should turn the scale.   Generous and passionate,
kind-hearted and vain, full of animal spirits and wil-
ful caprices, her character was that of April weather.
If occasion served, she was capable of the sublimest
things; if opportunities played her false, either by
thwarting her wishes or wounding her vanity, there
was no foreseeing what she might or might not do.
On learning from her father the honour that had
been conferred upon her, she blushed a little, then
smiled.   She was pleased, of course; neither did the
thought that all her dear girl-friends would turn
yellow with jealousy much lessen her pleasure.   But
she saw the finger of Colin Grainerau in this piece
of work, and, unlike her father, laid no more to the
account of Providence than strictly belonged to it.

It cannot be said that she much loved Grainereau,
or indeed, loved him at all, though she had agreed
to be his wife.   Grainereau was twice her age, and
neither good-looking, well-tempered, nor generous.
Nature fabricates a hundred thousand such peasants
as he every day, and scatters them about the world
to serve as examples of what are popularly known
as rural virtues.   The virtues of C. Grainereau consisted in his never giving a sou to anybody.   If
he saw his way to making fivepence he would go.

five miles to do it.   On Sundays he went to mass,
if he had the time; and on Mondays he always
found the time to take in somebody at the cattle-
market.   Personally, C. Grainereau stood five feet
four—out of his stockings, for he never wore any.
His face was of the colour and aspect of a medlar,
and his nose narrowed to a point from the centre of
it, like that of an American beast called the tapir.
To hear C. Grainereau talk was like listening to two
pieces of dried wood creaking together on a rusty
hinge; and, to square the list of his salient traits,
the man chewed tobacco and expectorated the
brown juice thereof at duly marked intervals in the
course of conversation.   But the particular virtue
that had decided Félicie to give him her hand was
his wealth, for he was rich, and it was no mean
offer for a dowerless girl like her to become mistress
of Grainereau Farm.   This she knew, and the ill-
concealed envy of her affectionate friends would
have taught it her if she hadn't.   Ah! if Yves Lallouette had been able to give his daughter a marriage portion!—then it would have been a different
story, and Colin Grainereau, to use the graceful
country term, might have gone back to his home and
whistled.   But poor Yves, though he earned sufficient in selling flowers, spent more than sufficient
in swilling white wine; and so the alternative lay

between marrying C. Grainereau and his "quinze mille livres de rentes," or going farther to fare probably worse. No French girl could hesitate, nor did Mdlle. Félicie. Still, self-esteem was so strong in her woman's heart, that she would have been glad to persuade herself that she was a little fond of C. Grainereau, and now and then she would con over in her mind whether he had not some rag of a quality which, by trying very hard, she might manage to love. His getting her elected Rosière afforded her the pretext she wanted. Decidedly C. Grainereau must have noble instincts. It did not suit Mdlle. Félicie any more than it suits other young ladies to suspect that there were any mercenary calculations in her lover's attentions. She much preferred to think that her own bright eyes had done it all; and in this instance there was every appearance of reason on her side, for what could her Rosière's dower signify to a man with "quinze mille livres," as above said? So C. Grainerau had evidently used his influence on her behalf solely out of love and chivalrous devotion. She felt grateful to him for it, and found him rather less ugly than usual when on the morrow of the election he called alone to offer his congratulations, attired in a waistcoat with blue glass buttons and a coat too tight under the arm-pits.

As for C. Grainereau himself, finding his love affairs and his monetary prosper so well, he was as near good-humour as his peculiar idiosyncrasy allowed. To the surprise of the neighbourhood, he treated somebody to a bottle of wine, of which he drank half: and in an unguarded moment was nearly giving a beggar a penny. After all let us do the man justice; he would have married Félicie if she had not possessed a centime. His getting her elected Rosière was an after-thought. If he could succeed in doing it, reflected he, the trousseau would cost him nothing, no more would the re-furnishing of the farm; and he *did* succeed, because in municipal councils such men as Grainereau take the lead, as progress demands they should. Once the matter settled, Grainereau turned his attention to the means how it might be made the most pro-fitable. In ordinary years the Rosière received the 500 francs which the bequest allowed; a gold watch and chain with pair of ear-rings from the municipal council, and the proceeds of a collection made in church. C. Grainereau fancied this might be im-proved upon. He moved in the council that the father of the Rosière be privileged every year to erect a marquee for dancing, and charge what he pleased at the entrance, the net receipts to be divided equally between him and the commune.

A day or two later, when his motion had been carried, C. Grainereau pointed out that it would be
unduly hard to call upon the Rosière for half her
profits, and suggested that a quarter would do. The
next day, having again succeeded, he returned to
the charge with the motion that it would be more
magnanimous to take nothing at all; and this
amendment having been voted like others — not,
however, without desperate resistance on the part
of the Opposition, who evinced sentiments utterly
beneath contempt — he successively obtained that
the Rosière's father should have a refreshment
license given him for the festal day, that the
dancing marquee should be erected, not at the
Rosière's expense, but at that of the commune, and
that the lighting of the said marquee should also
be provided for out of the communal funds. "We
can reform all that next year," reflected honest
Grainereau, "but there's no harm in the arrangement for once in a way."

The foregoing particulars, I should state, only
came to my knowledge at a later date, but I have
given them here for greater clearness. When Floriant,
myself, and party landed at Champterre we knew
no more of the Rosière than we had casually heard
on our way down, and we were none of us sorry to
find a squad of village boys retailing photographs of

the day's heroine at twenty sous a-piece. Before I forget it, let me mention that these photographs were also a device of Grainereau's. The worthy fellow had gone to a photographer, struck a bargain for the exclusive right to sell portraits of Félicie Lallouette in her Rosière dress, and pocketed three hundred francs on the transaction. So the village boys cried out at the top of their shrill voices, "Demandez la tête de Mam'selle Félicie!" and we each bought three or four of the heads in different attitudes, vignette, full face, and profile, and very fascinating heads they were. A pert, oval face it was, with rich masses of brown hair surmounting it; hazel eyes, with long sweeping lashes, good teeth, and a curious expression, half bold, half innocent; but innocent because youthful, as a young lioness might be who has never yet sucked blood, or a growing kitten before he has begun to filch cream. "Take my word for it," muttered Cirobois, with more reflectiveness than it was his wont to show. "We shan't have seen the last of this face to-day. It'll turn up some time or other and do something." With which prediction he and Braungesicht, being arm-in-arm as usual, stalked on ahead of us towards the church.

Heavens, what a crowd! The service had already begun and we squeezed in as we could, neither expecting a seat nor getting one. The

choristers were at their posts, twelve little fellows
with scarlet cassocks and lace surplices chaunting
to the music of a double-bass and an ophicleïde,
and making the quaint rhythm of their hymnal peal
clear as crystal under the old rafters of the chancel.
In seats of honour near the altar-rails, Mayor Parbouillaud, in his gold-fringed, tricolour sash, and his
council all rigged out in their Sunday best, not excluding the Opposition, who, although adverse to
the whole proceedings on principle, came to the
service in order to qualify for the dinner which took
place at 6.30. Opposite to the council as many
distinguished functionaries—justices of the peace,
commissary of police, and such kind—as could be
crammed into one pew; and in the most conspicuous
spot, midway between the two rows of seats and
right in the centre of the nave, three chairs placed
side by side, that to the right for the Rosière, that
to the left for the Rosière of the preceding year,
who, by a graceful fiction, was supposed to have
brought her successor to the present honour by the
shining force of example, and that in the middle
for the patroness of the fête, who this year chanced
to be the Prefect's wife—a brilliant lady, in a gown
couleur jonquille, whose task it was to lay the
coronet of roses on the Rosière's virginal brow, and
whisper to her a few graceful nothings.

Right down the length of the nave, the space was filled by seven and sixty firemen in brass helmets, blue swallow-tails with red facings, and pantaloons *ad libitum:* none other these than the famous *Pompiers de Champterre*, renowned in song as extinguishers of fires in the houses of men and igniters of flames in the hearts of women. At the head of them glowed their trusty captain, in private life a baker, whose gold epaulets stood out so fiercely on either side of his ears, that they looked as if they were going to fly away with his head, which was a small and mild one. M. le Curé, in his richest stole, MM. les Vicaires in their purple and gold chasubles, and Monsieur the Precentor, in his silver-rimmed spectacles, served to complete a bright picture, which was not inaptly capped by the beadle, whose flaming baldric, steel halbert, pink silk calves, and towering three-cornered hat, seemed to symbolize the antiquated features of the ceremony which he was there to grace.

But antiquated or not, the proceedings showed no lack of life, and you may think what you please, but when the crowning moment of the solemnity arrived, the sight was a really pretty—I was going to say a touching—one. Mass was over. The last prayers had been said. M. le Curé had feelingly and thumpingly delivered his sermon in three points on the praise of virtue. Everybody had sat down, rustled, and then stood up again, and the organist was softly playing a voluntary. Then there was a lull. Six little mites of girls dressed all in white emerged from the Virgin's chapel and toddled gravely up the nave, carrying three cushions between them. On the first cushion was the Rosière's crown, on the second a white satin purse containing her dower, and on the third a little jeweller's-box with the municipal gold watch and chain and the ear-rings in it. I thought, and still think, that to try and foster virtue by developing in it a taste for trinkets, is at least a bold experiment that must lead occasionally to unforeseen results. But innovations suggested by the modern spirit of liberality and progress are things so eminently respectable, that one must accept them with faith, notwithstanding internal misgivings, and so I say nothing against the municipal box. The little people with their cushions threaded their way along the bristling lane which the valiant firemen formed, reached their stand-point, dropped a curtsy, and ranged themselves in a semicircle opposite the patroness of the fête. Then this lady, assisted by Mayor Parbouillaud, who now gallantly bustled forward, rose, faced the congregation, and smilingly beckoned to the Rosière to approach. We then saw Mdlle. Félicie

Lallouette kneel on a hassock at the feet of Madame
la Préfète, who very prettily and rather blushingly
helped her to put on her chain and ear-rings; then
took the chaplet from its cushion and set it on her
head. This was a signal for the baker-captain of
the firemen corps, whose face had been convulsively
working like that of a man who has a public duty
to perform, and who at the precise moment when
the chaplet touched Mdlle. Félicie's hair, screamed
out in a voice that cracked right in the middle
from emotion: "Present arms!" Simultaneously the
organist touched his keys and pealed out the strains
of a triumphal march, whilst the Curé, bending over
the still kneeling girl, raised his hands aloft and
gave the benediction. This was the end. With a
great rush from all sides of the church, the congregation pressed forward to see the Rosière as she
walked out processionally. First came the firemen
headed by the baker, who marked time most satis-
factorily when the throng prevented his advancing;
then the beadle, then the Rosière herself, leaning
on the arm of the Mayor, and escorted by the six
little mites who strewed flowers on her path, then
the Préfète with her arm on that of worthy Yves
Lallouette, overwhelmed with the sense of so much
honour; then the municipal councillors, headed by
honest Colin Grainereau in a new waistcoat, and

with a fixed grin on his countenance; lastly, more
firemen to close up. And everybody who had a
rose in his button-hole, and every woman or girl
who had a nosegay in her hand, threw it as this
goodly procession filed by; so that soon the flags
were littered with rose-leaves as thick as a Turkey
carpet. My rose went with the rest, so did that of
Braungesicht, who regretted that he had not two
roses—nay, a whole basketful. As for Cirobois, he
only threw one single leaf of his, muttering as he
did so in the dry, peculiar tone that always left one
uncertain whether he was joking or not: "Trop de
fleurs, jeune fille, trop de fleurs! On commence par
là; on finit par les épines!" At this juncture I
turned round to look for Floriant. He had not
spoken during the ceremony. He was standing by
my side gazing chancelwards, and appearing to take
an interest altogether new to him in the proceedings.
For once in a way, I believe he positively forgot to
cast around him that sweeping and scrutatory glance
which Frenchmen of his age throw, pretty much as
a fisherman jerks his net, to see whether there are
any presentable women within eye-reach. He also
omitted either to stroke his moustache or finger his
satin scarf, which, under other circumstances, I
should have taken as an indication that he did not
feel well, or had lost more money than he liked at

baccarat. When the cortége began to move in our direction he slightly shifted his position, and gave vent to one of those murmured exclamations that do not mean much if a man is wont to express his sentiments by continual "Oh!'s" and "Ah!'s," but which signify a good deal in the mouth of a man whom a long acquaintance with wonders of all sorts has rendered reticent. Floriant had seen too many pretty women in his lifetime to be stirred by the sight of a new face, however striking; and yet as the Rosière neared us, he drew the flower from his button-hole, waited his opportunity, and when she was but a couple of yards distant from him, dropped it at her feet. The thing was done with infinite grace, but was so marked, that it was impossible to confound this particular flower with the others, or the donor of it with the rest of the throng. Mdlle. Félicie raised her eyes a little timidly, and bowed; and the Marquis de Floriant returned her salute with an inclination of the head, such as he habitually reserved for duchesses. All this was the work of a moment; then, apparently satisfied with his performance, Gaston took my arm and said: "And now what shall we do until ball time?"

III.

There was something of a problem in the question, for between the church service which we had just seen, and the ball which we were resolved to see, lay a bleak tract of eight hours, which could scarcely be filled to our own satisfaction by going to see the clodhoppers of Champterre climb their greasy poles for legs of mutton, or race in sacks for live rabbits. Cirobois counselled that we should invite the municipal council to luncheon, make them drunk, and then call upon them for an outspoken statement as to their views in politics. He had once, he averred, beguiled time in this way on the commune of his own estate down in Languedoc, and after two hours' champagning, had obtained from his council the most solemn declaration that they were a set of imbeciles. Unfortunately, the rate-leviers of Champterre would probably get drunk that day without our assistance, and at their own—or rather the rate-payers'—expense, so there was nothing for it but to adjourn to the one decent inn in the place, and order a repast, which, by smoking, anecdoting, and mixture of cool drinks, was eked out until the hour when respectable people think of dinner. About this time Floriant vanished, and did not turn up

again until close upon nine o'clock, when the streets
of the village were already lighted, when the fun in
the fair-booths was growing fast and furious, and
when from the vast marquee which Colin Grainereau
had caused to be erected for Yves Lallouette, his
future father-in-law, issued the *queak-queak* of fiddles
and the *toot-toot* of cornopeans being turned for the
evening's fray. Our party had been wandering about
in a desultory way, raffling for macaroons, shooting
down wax images for unsmokable cigars, and otherwise enjoying ourselves since seven. When the
marquee was thrown open we streamed in like one
man, and it was then that Floriant burst anew upon
our sight, arrayed in faultless evening-dress, with
diamond studs in his shirt-front, his hair curled, and
an opera-hat under his arm. He had gone back in
stealth to Paris to effect this revolution in his costume, and now confronted us with a smiling "I spilt
some wine over my waistcoat at luncheon, and so
was obliged to change. Once in Paris, I thought I
might as well dress, since there was going to be
dancing."

"But *you* are not going to dance?" asked Ra-
vignan of the Cent-Gardes, laughing.

"Look at these boards, man," giggled Narcisse
de Parabère, who often led the cotillon at the Court

balls; "there's an inch and a half between them. Have you insured your ankles?"

"Diamond studs, too!" lisped René de Morange, in a half-whisper to Cirobois. "When Floriant dresses like a snob, there's always some reason for it. He has set those diamonds to catch somebody—they are bird-lime."

"Or paste," suggested Cirobois. "Are you really going to show these bumpkins that you can hop almost as well as they?" added he, touching Floriant's arm.

"Bah! you will all of you dance," retorted Floriant. "And as to the clothes, they will be what everybody else will wear, except yourselves—so I shall be less remarked than you."

So far as that went, he was not quite wrong. Colin Grainereau had caused to be set up at the door a notice to this effect:

"ADMISSION, 5 FRANCS.

"*Well-wishers of the Rosière may give more if they please. By paying forty francs, gentlemen may obtain a pink ticket, which will entitle them to dance with the Rosière.*"

And this announcement had kept away all such Champterrians as were feeble folk, with no money in their purses. Further, C. Grainereau had set a detective from Paris to watch at the doors, and see that no ladies of a certain nameless category crept

in; and, thanks to these precautions, the gathering
was really as select as could be desired. All the
officials of the canton were there—they, their wives,
and their marriageable offspring. Local commerce
had its representatives; so had the garrison of the
neighbouring post-town; and, what with the white
neckcloths of the tradesmen, the councillors, and two
bald-headed churchwardens, and the red trousers of
three or four sub-lieutenants, very spruce in their
trim regimentals, Floriant's get-up did not seem so
much out of place as his admirers might have feared.
Nevertheless, it is useless to disguise that his studs
excited attention. The two bald churchwardens cast
glances of esteem at him; the councillors who passed
by made themselves respectfully small, so as not to
brush him with their elbows; awe fell upon the
waiter, who served him with a glass of seltzer-water;
and by-and-by, when he whirled round the room
waltzing with Mdlle. Félicie Lallouette, the poor girl
seemed unable to lift her eyes off the shiny stones,
in which surely the devil must have elected his
abode for that evening.

It appeared to me when Mdlle. Félicie entered
the ball-room that she had grown a good year older
since the morning, not only in age but in experience.
Truth to say, that is a trying ordeal which takes a
young girl from the secluded innocency of home,

and places her of a sudden into a glaring position, where she becomes for a day the queen of her neighbourhood, the admired object of all eyes, the recipient of a thousand flatteries, none the less dangerous because spoken out in plain round terms, with bucolic frankness. Then, Mdlle. Félicie had been chief guest at the municipal dinner that evening, and, if facts must be told as they are, champagne corks had been popped with a prodigality only known at those banquets where it is not the poppers who pay. Mdlle. Félicie had never tasted it before, and this time she had tasted it to an extent that made her beautiful eyes beam like Scotch cairngorms, her breath go quicker, and cheeks glow like August peaches. Unfortunate C. Grainereau! what infatuation can have possessed him under such auspices as these to show himself to his betrothed with his weasly face, his preposterous garments, his walnut-coloured hands, and his ploughman's gait? With a face like his, the man ought to have hidden himself under a bushel for the day, and only reappeared when, the pomp and glitter of the festivity being over, he would have had no comparison to dread with any of the brilliant butterflies who were fluttering round his Félicie. As it was C. Grainereau looked like an unclean beetle gadding about a white tablecloth; and, to add to his natural charms, he had drunk himself into hiccoughs and unsteadiness. What chance could he have against the Marquis de Floriant? It seemed that Floriant had bought up all the tickets that gave the holders right to dance with the Rosière. At all events, after the first quadrille, which she opened with Mayor Parbouillaud, and the first polka, which she footed with the mild baker-captain of the firemen corps, nobody, not even C. Grainereau himself, could obtain a dance from her. C. Grainereau probably consoled himself with the reflection that, having honestly issued more pink tickets than there were dances for, the purchasers would find their bargains less profitable than they had hoped. But this he only thought for the early part of the evening. As the hours wore on, and it was always the same purchaser who danced with his Rosière, as polka followed quadrille, and waltz polka, and still it was that same young blade, with the diamond buttons and the waxed moustache, C. Grainerau's features became discomposed. I think I perceived the precise moment when suspicion first flashed across him. He was leaning vinously and complacently against one of the tent-poles, brewing heaven knows what thoughts in his crooked mind, when the Marquis passed with Félicie into the refreshment-room, close to him—so close, indeed, that Félicie could not but have perceived him, though she gave no token of the fact except by turning her head, purposely as it seemed, the other way. In the refreshment-room, Yves Lallouette, who had been plied with congratulatory drink ever since sunrise (and it was now within an hour of midnight), sat hopelessly rooted to a chair, with his purple face blinking unconsciously at nothing. His daughter stopped before him, however, and seemed to be whispering who her partner was. He staggered to his feet, held out a rocking hand, drivelled something about the "honour," etc., and floundered backwards again. Floriant and the Rosière then sat down at an adjoining table, whither anon rushed a waiter with an iced pail of Cliquot. At this moment the flower-girl, Mirabelle, glided into the room, being, apparently, a privileged person, free to enter everywhere. She looked round as if seeking somebody, perceived where Floriant was, and smiled a rather meaning smile. She made towards him, holding the bouquet she had promised to keep that morning, and, dropping a curtsy, said, "I was sure you would want it, Monsieur le Marquis."

Floriant took the bouquet, of course, and handed it to Mdlle. Félicie, and it was then that, crossing the room, and chancing to light upon the features of C. Grainereau, I noted the ghastly change they underwent. The man clapped his hand to his forehead, gave a gasp, and was sobered in one instant.

Most of us—I mean we good-for-noughts who had come down from Paris—had been dancing. It was the custom, said one of our number. We should look singular if we didn't. It was not fair, coming to a ball, to act as kill-joys; and so on. In short, we danced. But on beholding the grimace which C. Grainereau pulled, and the direction which his thunder-laden glances took, I guessed there was a storm preparing; nor was I wrong.

Cirobois was near me, mystifying his Prussian with an account of some French provincial customs, which Braungesicht was listening to attentively with the most guileless faith. I confided my apprehensions to him. "Oh yes," he answered quietly; "I have been looking for the storm this long while. We had better keep an eye on the pair—that's all we can do."

"But I shall go and warn Floriant."

"Breath's precious: better not waste it. There are three things you can never stop: a train flying downhill, a joint-stock company going to grief, and a woman on the slope to———"

He did not finish, for Floriant had just conducted Félicie Lallouette back to her place, and was taking leave of her. In doing so, he stooped, said something that evidently pleased her, causing her both to smile and to redden; and in shaking hands with her, held her hand within his own just a short second longer than there was any need for. Then bowing in a way that said in the clearest dumb language possible, "*Au revoir*," and not "*Adieu*," he withdrew. Colin Grainereau uttered a sort of growl, clenched his fists, rushed into the refreshment-room, and swallowed a glass of brandy to give himself courage, and then followed him.

"Now for the storm!" remarked Cirobois; and we went out too.

There was a crowd outside listening to the music; but beyond the throng Floriant was discernible in the grey overcoat which he had donned, lighting a cigar, and seemingly making his way to the station.

"Stop!" screamed Grainereau, running after him; and in a paroxysm of passion he caught Floriant by the shirt-front, shook him savagely, and yelled: "Go away from here, do you hear me? go away, and never come near us again!"

Floriant had been taken aback; but recovering from his surprise, he caught the unlucky peasant roughly by the throat, swayed him, and sent him reeling ten yards away. Our timely arrival prevented further hostilities. We ran between the two, and asked Grainereau by name (for he had been pointed out to us several times over that day) what he meant.

But, as is the way with countrymen, all the man's valour had forsaken him upon finding that he was not the strongest; and at our question, instead of firing up anew, he lapsed maudlin, put his hands to his eyes, and whined: "Why should he come here and turn her head? What has she done to him, and what harm have *I* ever done him?" spluttered he, piteously. "I should make her happy, and he knows I would. There are enough women in that Paris of his—why does he not go and take one of them?" Before we could foresee his intention, he bundled himself down on his knees, embraced Floriant's legs with his arms, and cried: "Hark you, young rich man! you shall have all the money of your tickets back again, if you will go. I watched her with you this evening, and you've turned her head. You have. I saw it in her eyes, and I tell you it's a bad action—a bad action!" roared he two or three times over, and he continued to snivel and whimper.

"You're drunk; let me go!" exclaimed Floriant, impatiently, and he shook himself free.

Colin Grainereau got up blubbering, and tottered to a lamp-post, for his tipsiness seemed to have got the better of him again. He pressed his forehead against the cold iron, and sobbed, half from drunkenness, half with impotent rage and grief.

We four walked on in silence; but at the first turning of the road, Cirobois stopped, and laid a hand on Floriant's shoulder.

"Look here, old fellow," he said, with some earnestness in his voice, and looking Floriant fixedly in the face, "take my advice and *don't*. Nothing good can come of it."

IV.

Two or three years passed. Within a week of the Rosière's fête circumstances had drawn me away from Paris, and when I returned I learned that Floriant had gone travelling, but with whom, for whom, or for what, people were much too busy with their own concerns to inquire. One day, however, passing near the Paris corn-market, I met a wizen face which I could just remember having seen somewhere. It was the face of an ugly, ·melancholy, and cross-grained looking farmer, in a wide-awake hat and a white blouse. He seemed to recognize me, for without being spoken to he addressed me, hissing and pale with sudden passion: "I've not forgotten your face nor *his*, and if you see him you may tell him so. May heaven curse him! If I meet him again it won't be fists I shall try on him, no, nor wood. You may tell him that too!" And he trudged onwards, mumbling threatening oaths. The only explanation I could find to which enigma was that Colin Grainereau—for my interlocutor was he—had got drunk again.

But the circumstance had not quite slipped from my memory when, some weeks later, my servant entered whilst I was at my breakfast and announced, "Le Marquis de Floriant."

I liked Floriant, and though we never wrote to each other when separated, our acquaintanceship was not one of those that are slackened by absence. I was glad to see him, and in less than five minutes both of us were at table talking as old friends again. Perhaps, indeed, these are the pleasantest friendships, which one can lay down and take up anew without inconvenience on either side.

"And so you are only just returned to Paris, Floriant?"

"Only just, and my first visit is for you."

"You must have roamed the whole world over— Egypt, India, Japan?"

"No, nothing further than Italy—Rome, Venice, the old story. We travel, and find the only city worth living in is Paris."

"And yet the time has passed pleasantly?"

"Yes, oh yes." And this answer meant no, as most such replies do.

We adjourned to the balcony for coffee and to smoke. Floriant remained some minutes silent, and I had leisure to observe that he was altered—thinner, paler, and more thoughtful-looking. But he no longer seemed *blasé*, and his dress, though correct and tasteful, was not the distressingly elaborate thing of former days. After wreathing a few clouds into the air, he suddenly laid down his cigar, drew his chair closer to mine, and said, very impressively, "I am going to ask a favour of you, Blamont."

"Ask," I answered, a little astonished, but with a smile.

"Well, it's a matter that can only be undertaken by a friend of proved discretion," explained he, with growing excitement discernible in his manner. "I want you to negotiate a 'break-off' for me," and he drew a sigh as though to say, "Now the thing's out."

"Are there letters to get back—or what?"

"No, no letters, but it will be uphill argument. She loves me, I believe, tenaciously, almost savagely; I don't love her, and I have a marriage in view. You see I am thirty now. A man can't spend his whole life driving up and down the Champs Elysées, nodding to women he doesn't care for, and losing his money at horse-races. I think I perceive my way to doing something in politics or diplomacy;

and my marriage may help me.   You'll see her. She is charming—an Italian, first-rate family, plenty of money—which is a secondary consideration—but sweet-tempered and pretty as an angel . . . ."

"Who, the person you want to break with?"

"Oh no, the other—the one I want to marry. This second one, she's pretty too—yes; but you can't understand what it is to be tied to a woman with whom you have no community of thought. It's like the shot chained to the convict's ankle; and I've been undergoing this for more than two years—an eternity!" He positively moaned as he said this, and his next words almost took the form of an entreaty: "You'll offer anything she pleases, Blamont, to break off with me—that is, not to do anything to thwart my marriage; for she could thwart it if she would, and I am sure she would do it if not argued with.   I have been having her trained for the stage, so that she might have a paying profession to fall back upon; but you must say I'll make over twelve thousand francs a year to her in Rentes if she will go and live out of France—in Belgium, or Switzerland, or some such place.   She shall have double if she wishes it—anything, so that she break, for good and all."

He rambled on for a considerable while to this effect—for it was really little better than rambling;

and I could not help admiring the retributive justice of the Nemesis which had overtaken such a Lothario as Floriant, by putting him in the power of an importunate, uneducated woman, whom he dreaded, and on whose nod or refusal the whole of his future career seemed to hinge. When he had favoured me with a whole host of particulars essential to the success of the negotiations, and coached me with diplomatic hints enough to have led him with flying colours out of any creditable undertaking, he was for having me start at once and get the business settled out of hand. Up to this moment he had not breathed a word as to the woman's name or her antecedents, so I questioned him on this subject.

He seemed on the point of telling me, then hesitated, and at length exclaimed, "No, go straight and see her, that's the best way; you've met her once in your life," and upon this he thrust a card with an address upon it into my hands and ran out, leaving me to make of his explanations what I could.

The embassy was not a very agreeable one, but friendship is exposed to be sent on missions of this kind, and to be little thanked into the bargain whether they succeed or fail. So I took a cab and drove to an hotel near the Bois de Boulogne, much resorted to by people who wished to imagine themselves in the country while being in Paris. I was shown up a sagaciously carpeted—I was going to say muffled—staircase, through corridors embellished with reproductions of sculptured masterpieces in simili-marble and so on into a drawing-room commanding a view of a garden, where some rather flashy guests of the hotel were lunching. The lady was not in the room; but the waiter vanished to apprise her maid; and whilst he was gone, I was able with a glance or two to reconnoitre the chamber and all its appurtenances. On the table, amidst a medley of women's knick-knacks, were one or two rehearsal-books of Boulevard comedies then in vogue; at another part of the table an open copy-book, which I had not the indiscretion to examine, but which at a distance looked curiously like an exercise-ground for pothooks and hangers. On a chair a grammar.

I had been perhaps five minutes in the room when silk rustled down the passage. The door was flung open, and a woman of superb beauty rushed in rather impetuously, as if she well knew the person she expected to meet. On seeing me, however, she stopped, looked at me astonished, and, then, with somewhat of a tremor in her voice, like that which comes of a presentiment of evil, asked me to what she was indebted for the pleasure of my visit. The woman was Félicie Lallouette.

She had never known me, however, and so had no occasion to colour at any untimely recollections. But she suspected evil, and I can see her now leaning on the arm of the chair into which she had thrown herself, resting her chin on her hand, and turning her large, liquid eyes on me waiting for an explanation. She was no longer the Félicie of three years ago. Time had added to her beauty while changing the character of it. It was now a haughty beauty—that of a woman of passion who has braved the world and feels the need to hold her head high, to assert a position which she knows is not hers. In good sooth, I am no admirer of the unsexed class into which she had drifted, but I pitied the woman, and in telling her on what errand I had come, conveyed my message with all the forbearance and delicacy that I had at command. She listened without answering a word, but her hands turned to marble as I was speaking, and her face looked like that of a statue. The only live part in her features were her eyes, and they, instead of deadening, changed to fire, glowing with quietly suppressed intensity, that had something terrifying in it. She waited until I had quite finished, then sat a moment motionless. After which she rose and said coldly:—

"And what does he expect?"

"Expect that you will be amenable to reason and prudence," I answered gently.

"Never," she said, with defiant firmness.

This "never" was like the closing of an iron door. I have heard such emphatic "nevers" on one or two other occasions during my life, and every time I have felt, what I then felt, that though it was a woman who spoke, the case was hopeless.

"But what do you intend doing?" I inquired.

"I intend to break with him," was her calm reply. "I would never accept a centime more of his money if I were starving of hunger. I shall leave him, but not free to do what he pleases and break others' lives as he has broken mine. He swore to me that he loved me, did your friend, swore it hundreds upon hundreds of times, and I believed him. What is this code of morality which suffers a nobleman to perjure himself to a woman, and yet deem himself honourable and a fit mate for an innocent girl? I am not of your sphere of society, Monsieur, but what little I have been able to learn of its ways since your friend raised me or lowered me from the station where I stood, has taught me that the one law it places above all others, is respect for plighted faith. I cannot conceive that this law makes exceptions and says: 'You shall keep your word to all save a woman.' So, as your friend has deceived me, I have a right to conclude he will deceive others; and it shall be my business to prevent him, *if I can*, from making new victims."

This was said without declamation, quietly and coldly.

"But what can you do?" I asked, disconcerted.

"Do?" she answered. "I will retire to the mire whence I sprung, with my innocence and my illusions the less, and a hatred in my heart the more. I will work for my bread—but whenever your friend hopes to link a trusting girl's destiny to his, or enter upon a career that promises honour or distinction, he will find me upon his path, and he will learn what a fallen woman's vengeance is."

I endeavoured to remonstrate, but with a quick, not undignified, wave of the hand, she cut me short.

"I have nothing more to add, Monsieur," she said, "but that I shall leave this within an hour." And upon this she touched the bell, thus signifying to me to bow and withdraw.

V.

"A woman's vengeance!" I thought, but this was some eighteen months afterwards, under widely different circumstances—that is, at Versailles, where I had been summoned to give evidence at the examination of a Pétroleuse.

It was in the bitterly raw June of the present
year.* The day was grey, with gusts of rain and
wind, and the weather seemed to render more
sinister and dank the lobby in which I, and some
score of other witnesses, were waiting our turns to
be examined. This was not a trial, but only a summary cross-questioning of the women who had been
seized red-handed, and imprisoned together at Sar-
tory, at the close of the insurrection. Gendarmes
with oil-skin over their hats, and heads bent down
to avoid the sleet that would have pelted into their
faces, clanked by every minute, leading handcuffed
women across a paved yard from the extemporized
prison to the court-house or back again. And what
women! No gleam of romance to be extracted from
those misshapen countenances; little sympathy, even,
that could be afforded to women so bereft of all
that renders woman lovable. I saw a batch of unfortunate creatures who had been arrested that very
morning in the slums of Paris, and were trudging along
chained to one another by the wrists. They did
not bear themselves with the dogged sullenness which
men show when in trouble. They laughed hysteri-
cally as they went, shrieked infamous songs, spat
out jeering insults against the soldiers who were
their escort; and one of them—a woman past middle-

* 1871.

age, in a silk gown, with the paint of her profession still on her—seeing me look through the window, pulled out her tongue and made a face at me. "Surely," thought I, "women, when they *do* fall, fall to fathomless depths." And I began to muse on whose behalf or against whom I could have possibly been called to bear testimony.

I was not long kept in doubt. A gendarme, reeking with wet, entered with a list in his hand, read out my name and address, and said, "This way, if you please."

I followed the man through a labyrinth of passages, which, notwithstanding that it was mid-day, were lit with flickering oil-lamps. On the floor, soldiers worn out with the fatigues of the past days were sleeping and snoring in exhausted attitudes. At every ten yards, stacks of arms; in every doorway, sentinels with bayonets fixed. The prison had been formerly a cavalry barrack, and the court-house whither my gendarme guide led me was a transformed saddle-room.

The door closed behind us, and I found myself in a whitewashed chamber, the walls of which were still adorned with pegs, where hung for the nonce military képis and sabres. At a deal table, encumbered with papers and pewter inkstands, half-a-dozen officers were sitting in undress uniforms. The Pre-

sident, a peremptory colonel, who wasted little time
in formalities, looked up as I appeared and, pointing
to a woman ignobly clad and deeply pitted with
small-pox, who stood behind a sort of bar, said,
"Monsieur, this woman is accused of having set fire
to the mansion of the Marquis de Floriant in the
Rue de Lille."

The woman nodded and drew a tattered shawl
closer round her. The gendarmes to right and left
of her frowned and looked indignant at her calmness.

"By profession," resumed the Colonel, "the
woman is—is—everything that these women are
when they cut the figure of this one; but she calls
herself an operative—says she was taken ill with
small-pox during the siege, and only joined the
Communalist insurrection for the purpose of burning
this single house down. As to name, she pretends
she has none—but she states that you know her,
and will answer for her being not a thief. We
have called you at her request."

I had hitherto been standing on the same line with
the woman, and had not caught a good sight of her
features. I now stepped in front of her, and looked at
her face—out of which, as behind a cloud, dimly rose
the recollection of lineaments seen but twice before.

"Yes," she said, nodding again simply, "it's me.
I wish you to say," added she, in an undisturbed

tone, "that I am—am not what the Colonel thinks. I worked for my bread, as I promised you I would: it is the small-pox that has made me ugly—that and poverty. Why I burned the Hôtel de Floriant, *you* know. I have prevented your friend's marriage. I have debarred him from ever wrecking the happiness of another girl as he did mine. I was wrong to burn his house, that I confess: but we do things in moments of bitterness that we would not do otherwise. Say to the gentleman that it was not to plunder, will you, that I did this . . .?"

It was not immediately that I could speak. I seemed to be seeing her before me that Sunday at Champterre, with the crown of white roses, the pealing of the organ, and the Curé's benediction.

"Monsieur," I faltered at last to the Colonel, "I swear this woman is to be pitied."

She bent her head in acknowledgment, and said, with just the slightest quaver in her voice, "Thank you, Monsieur."

The next thing I heard of her was that she had been condemned to death.

———

A HERO OF THE COMMUNE.

A HERO OF THE COMMUNE.

AN EPISODE OF 1871.

I.

SOME ten years ago, when people asked Monsieur Torreau, of the Rue Quincampoix, Paris, what he thought of doing with his son Jules, who was then a lanky youth, with trousers too short for him, M. Torreau used to answer, in a tone of voice and with a toss of the head such as could only have come from a retired hatter who had got "dix milles livres de rente," that Jules was destined to become a Government functionary. And you should have heard the stress he laid upon that word FUNCTIONARY! Young Jules insensibly loomed upon the imagination of the listener attired in golden swallow-tails, with a red ribbon round his throat, a touch of lumbago, a pair of spectacles over his eyes, and a roll of administrative parchment under his arm. I think it was a secret chagrin to both the worthy people, M. and Mdme. Torreau, that their son was such a long time getting bald. They looked with tender impatience to the day when his head, denuded of its hirsute forest, should shine like a new-laid egg, when his girth should round itself into the decorous shapeliness of a pumpkin, and when he should reap his visage every morning, leaving nought but moustache and "imperial" to denote that he was a man in authority, holding Bonapartist convictions, and enjoying a salary out of the public taxes. Alas! best of parents, what would you have said had it been predicted to you that your offspring, Jules, would climb the steeps of power with a poll as shaggy as the uncombed mane of a lion, a beard flaming out to a foot's length on either side of his countenance, and the word "Republican" indelibly stamped on every part of his person and apparel— on his finger-nails, on the ragged cuffs and greasy collar of his coat, on the furious-looking brim of his wide-awake hat? Ah me! . . . . But let us not anticipate.

Young Jules was a good lad, and would have made a blameless hatter; but his father, with a restless eye to his future greatness, had sent him early to the Lycée Bonaparte, which was a mistake, for the Lycée Bonaparte in the Chaussée d'Antin was the most official and aristocratic of all the public schools; and when it became known there that young Jules was the son of "TORREAU, *inventor*

of the Simili-Panama, warranted to stand all weathers.
Price fifty sous. Beware of spurious imitations,"
the joke was thought too good a one to be lost, and
all the aristocratic young heads of "Bonaparte" blos-
somed out with simili-panamas, bought with hoarded
pocket-money, and indulged in criticisms on the bad-
ness of this head-dress, in the hearing of young
Jules, and with the kind intention of making him
foam at the mouth. But it must be recorded that
young Jules revenged himself with spirit. When the
thing had gone far enough, he flattened his fist on
the nose of a senator's son so vigorously as to keep
that young gentleman for two-and-twenty days on
the sick-list; with his boot he drove the heir of an
Envoy Extraordinary and Minister Plenipotentiary
rolling amidst a heap of plates; and, armed with a
simili-panama, he collared the rising hope of a Councillor of State, and made a furious, though happily
ineffectual, attempt to force the obnoxious covering
down his throat. After which, having established
his physical supremacy, he exclaimed, with his teeth
set, "And now I'll tell you what the son of a hatter
can do," and from that day forth won all the school-
prizes—all, without exception. At the annual so-
lemnities, when the rewards were distributed before
a concourse of friends and distinguished visitors, it
was invariably young Torreau's name that headed

the roll; and in the last year of his academic career, when he took part in the Concourse Général, which is a competition of all the public schools in Paris, he carried the "Prize of Honour,"—that for Latin Essay,—and enjoyed the triumph of being cheered to the echo by his old antagonists, who, proud of the lustre he was shedding on their school, shouted rapturously, "Vive Torreau!" and set up a hurricane of applause as, flushed and nervous amidst a vast assembly of spectators risen to their feet to do him honour, he descended from the daïs where he had received his crown of gilt laurel-leaves and his two thousand francs' worth of books from the Minister of Public Instruction.

I promise you that was a fine day for the Torreau connection. The excellent Madame Torreau wept a pocket-handkerchief-ful of tears; the face of Torreau senior looked like a freshly cooked lobster; and pretty Mdlle. Victorine Torreau, known in the Quartier Quincampoix as the future possessor of "cent mille livres de dot," was as pink with pleasure and as moist about the eyes as though she had been suffered to marry poor Celestin Joubarbe, her father's ex-apprentice, who had dared to aspire to her hand, and been ignominiously forbidden the house in consequence. But the climax was reached when, according to traditional usage, young Jules set out at

six o'clock in the evening to dine with his Excellency the Minister at the latter's official residence.
It was an event never to be forgotten in the Rue
Quincampoix. Mdme. Torreau had bought Jules a
gold watch and dazzling chain; Mdlle. Victorine
had hemmed him a dozen white cravats; an uncle
in the tailoring way had cut him a dress-suit out of
the most glossy cloth of Elbœuf; and a second
uncle, erst partner of Torreau senior, but now carrying on the simili-panama trade by himself, had presented him with a new opera-hat, patented, self-ex-
panding, and costing twenty-five francs. In all of
which splendours, and with his head as firmly im-
bedded in the starched folds of one of the cravats
aforesaid as if it had been screwed there, young
Jules burst upon the awe-stricken sight of his cab-
man and of the entire neighbourhood congregated
on their doorsteps to see him off. As for Torreau
senior, beside himself with contentment, he spent
the evening in regaling his good friend Bastien
Potachaux, ex-hosier and glover (whose son had won
no prize), with the story of what advantages were
attached to the Prix d'Honneur. And, truth to say,
these advantages almost constituted a fortune. Thus,
Jules would be exempted from military service. If
he elected to enter the Bar, he would be dispensed
from paying fees. If he chose to become a Profes-

sor, the École Normale was open to him. Or, if he
thought of turning Engineer or Artillery officer, he
was privileged to step straight into the École Polytechnique without passing the usual examinations.
"And he will adopt the latter course," concluded
Torreau senior, slapping the thigh of Bastien Potachaux, who listened with that natural enthusiasm
we always evince at hearing that our friends' children have earned honours which our own have been
unable to obtain. "He will join the Polytechnic
School next October, become a Government engineer;
and then, my old friend, one of these days, when
you and I have got no teeth left in our heads, we
shall see him Minister of Public Works, or perhaps
—who knows?—Prime Minister." Thus Torreau
senior, in the exuberance of his heart; and the
words were fulfilled as he had spoken, for in the
month of October following young Jules was admitted into the École Polytechnique, and attired
in the brass-buttoned coat, straight sword, and trim
cocked hat, which compose the uniform of that institution.

He remained a Polytechnician two years, and
during that time had conic sections hammered into
him by one professor, fortifications by a second,
chemistry by a third, and the gentle art of wrapping
one's head in wet towels the better to work all night

by a fourth. The École Polytechnique is a forcing-house, where the State endeavours to rear at great cost and with assiduous care that valuable plant called a *savant*. The better to do this, the State lays it down as a fundamental axiom that an amount of work which would kill a full-grown man outright need not interfere with the development of a growing boy. So the forcing is carried on at full steam, high pressure, and with all valves closed. The sprouting *savant* is kept to it morn, noon, and night, and bidden not forget that the eye of his country is upon him: the result of which is that if he do not prematurely collapse, the sprouting *savant* is restored to his affectionate family with his eyesight permanently weakened, his shoulders rounded, and a chronic singing in the head. Such was the fate of young Jules. After he had been at the school three months, being tenderly asked at home what he should like for a birthday present, he hinted at a pair of spectacles. At the end of half a year he gloomily directed his tailor to make his waistbands narrower. At the close of the twelvemonth he would occasionally complain that he felt something like a lump of lead inside his head; and on the day following the final examination he was laid up with brain-fever. But he had his reward. For when the lists were published his name was at the top; and the State, to recompense him for his noble efforts, for his two years of wet-towelling, and for his brain-fever, lost no time in appointing him to the post of fifth Government engineer in a remote town near the Pyrenees, at a salary of—eighty pounds a year.

II.

I remember, as if it were yesterday, the summer morning when young Jules dawned upon that town in the Pyrenees from the roof of a slow-paced diligence. It was the town at Touscrétins. I was secretary to the prefect, M. de Feucontenu, and overnight my chief had said to me: "There is that young Torreau expected here to-morrow, but as Monsieur Nul, the chief engineer, is absent with his staff cutting out the new road, perhaps you had better go and meet the young fellow, and help him to find lodgings."

So at daybreak I was standing in the yard of the "Lion d'Or," waiting for the diligence to come in.

It was always regarded as something of a sight, this coming in of the diligence, so that whilst the serving-maid of the "Lion d'Or" was laying out on the polished oil-cloth of the dining-room table the pyramids of white rolls, the pats of fresh-churned butter, and the large round bowls that were by-and-by to be filled with *café au lait* for such of the travellers as liked to breakfast there, a few of the local quidnuncs who were early risers, congregated beside me, with their pipes in their mouths and their hands in their pockets, to see if perchance there should be anything new that morning. Mdlle. Jeannine, the serving-maid, looked at them, laughing, through the dining-room window, and said to me: "They're always the same—regular at their posts like oysters on a sand-bank. If you came here three hundred and sixty-five days out of the year you'd always find them. But what brings *you* here so early?"

I explained my errand to the young lady, and told her I had come to meet a Polytechnician.

"Ah!" said she, "I don't like Polytechnicians."

"I am sorry for that, for I think of bringing this particular one to lodge here."

"Then that's another bed I shall have to make, that's all."

"Why don't you like Polytechnicians?"

"What is there to like in them? Gentlemen who walk bent double like compasses, and who are for ever proving things by rule, just as if it wasn't the stupidest thing in the world to go by rule! I don't like people who prove things. The Saint. Cyrians are much better. There's your friend, M.

de Gardefer of the Cuirassiers, who never knows what he says and is always laughing. He's much more amusing."

"And not bad-looking either, Mdlle. Jeannine?"

"I don't know anything about his looks—but chattering with you makes me lose time, M. Louis. There's the tooting of the diligence horn, too, and, mon Dieu! I've not yet put my milk on."

Amid great clouds of dust, with the bells of its six mules all jingling together, and the bluff voice of its Biscayan driver shouting *Hue! Hop la! Ho!* the massive vehicle came rumbling down the road, slackened its pace within sight of the inn, looked as if it would rock over when turned sharp opposite the courtyard, but righted itself without effort and rolled jolting over the paving-stones, through the gates, and so on up to the inn door, where everybody alighted. The passengers who slid off the top and released themselves from the inside were of the usual category. A fat man with a portmanteau and a sheaf of umbrellas, walking-sticks, and fishing-rods, who had had the *coupé* all to himself; a trio of pot-manu-facturers who had been talking earthenware all the way from the rival town of Tousabrutis; a young curate with a portentous mushroom hat, freshly ordained and nervous, who had essayed to strike up a mild conversation with a swarthy Provençal nurse in charge of a swarthy and squalling Provençal baby; and a brace of officers in mufti on the box, going back to garrison after furlough, and looking hugely bored. But all these travellers were of hale complexion, had pink faces, and more or less square shoulders: whence it was easy for a connoisseur to guess that none of them was young Torreau of the Government Forcing-House. I waited till I saw a washed-out physiognomy arise from amidst the boxes on the roof, and peer around it with an air of scrutiny, and when this physiognomy, preceded by a pair of interminable and angular, yet withal deliberate legs, had scrambled down the sides of the diligence like some black outlandish spider, I stepped forward and said, "Monsieur Torreau, I believe?"

"Yes," said he, "Torreau." And he fixed upon me one of the most curiously expressive pair of eyes I had ever seen before or have seen since.

"My name is Louis Blamont," I added, "and I am here to act as your cicerone; in fact, to render you any service in my power."

"You are very good," said he, and he began gravely to look about him for two very hard, corded, parallelogramic boxes that constitued his luggage; also for a mottled tin box, shaped like an isos-

celes triangle, and which presumably contained his
cocked-hat.

"I will tell one of the ostlers to carry these up
to your rooms," I suggested, observing him stoop
to lift the heaviest and stiffest of the parallelograms
himself.

"An ostler costs fivepence," was his discouraging
reply, "and the thing will be sooner and better done'
if I do it myself." And with some little straining'
he contrived to hoist the box on to his shoulders as'
a bargeman does a sack of coals, and staggered with'
it towards the inn. To humour his whim, and save'
his unfortunate thin legs another journey, I caught
up the second box and the isosceles triangle, and'
moved after him. "Here is an original character,"'
thought I, and, struck with the novelty of a Govern-'
ment functionary of two-and-twenty perspiring to
save fivepence, I watched with some curiosity to see
what he would do next. What he did next was to
carry his box to the very top of the house, on the
plea that the rooms on the lower storeys would be
too dear for him. Then he drove a hard bargain,
with the landlord of the "Lion d'Or," proved to him'
beyond power of refutation that the sum he had
first asked for was excessive, and triumphantly'
secured a reduction of thirty sous a week. After
which he extracted a new uniform from one of the'

parallelograms, and was about to retreat to his bed-room in order to put it on, when I stopped him by saying that if he purposed calling on the head engineer, his chief, he must wait till the morrow, as M. Nul and his subalterns were absent making the new road, four leagues off, and would not be back till evening.

"Well, I'll go and join them," said young Tor-reau, in a matter-of-fact way, without pausing to debate the question with anybody.

"On a sweltering day like this, walk twelve kilo-mètres!" I protested. "Come, come!"

"I know it's hot," answered he, significantly wiping the perspiration from his brow, "but Govern-ment is not going to give me a salary to take notes about the weather. Besides, I suspect the workmen who are cutting the road, find it quite as hot as I do."

"But you have not yet breakfasted," I remon-strated, "and I was just going to invite you."

"Oh, as to breakfast," said he, "I can buy a piece of bread and eat it going along."

And so he did, and set off on the spot, in an undress uniform, and with metrical implements under his arm, I escorting him, and acting as his guide. We went a kilomètre together, and there I left him. He had not spoken a dozen words the whole way, but had munched his crust and taken such formidable strides, that I returned in the same condition as if I had been in a vapour-bath. Breakfast had just been served at the prefecture, and I was in time to subside into my seat, and be asked whether I had been running a race, or doing anything else extraordinary.

"Well, and our new comer," added M. de Feucontenu, "does he promise to be an addition to our circle?"

"I hope he waltzes," remarked Madame la Préfète, whose one preoccupation was the success of her Wednesday *Thé-Dansants*.

"And does he look as if he could play billiards?" asked Raoul de Gardefer, a sort of cousin of Madame la Préfète's, and tolerably regular in his attendance at our board.

I tried to describe what manner of a man young Torreau was; but toned down the colours rather, for being fresh from seeing the original, who had not impressed me as a very brilliant picture, I preferred he should have the chance of being judged on his own merits whenever he put in his appearance at the prefecture. What I said, however, was enough to make Madame de Feucontenu understand that he did not convey the idea of being a very enthusiastic waltzer, and Raoul de Gardefer that, what-

ever taste he might possess for billiards, he was n
likely to bestow much money on that pastim
Madame la Préfète sighed, and Lieutenant de Ga
defer gave a shrug. As for the Prefect, he opine
with a grin, that young Torreau's anxiety to be qui
at work would wear off in time, as such indust
generally did, and he was good-natured enough
point this remark, gathered from his profound e
perience of subalterns, at me. On the whole it w
decided that young Torreau should have a card f
the next Dancing Tea, and there be put through ;
the social ordeals, one after the other.

But several days before the Dancing Te
mysterious rumours began to circulate about tl
town. It should be premised that Touscrétins w
not used to emotions of any sort: it did not li]
them, it would have nothing to say to them.
a general way it was a peaceful town, fond
order, and paying its taxes. It also greatly 1
spected the Government. Such men as thrived
other places, journalists and the like, had no hc
there: they withered up by the roots and perish
miserably. There was indeed a legend, purporti
that at some time or other, vaguely undefined,
misguided individual had tried to start an oppo
tion paper at Touscrétins, but it was only a leger
Serious people declined to believe that such a ve

15*

ture could have been possible, and even the authors
of the legend acknowledged that the editor, after
selling one copy of his first and last impression, departed from the town at nightfall indebted to his
printer, and was never heard of again. Touscrétins
was not likely to miss him. There was that in the
town's very appearance which suggested constituted
authority, and the inborn, unlimited worship of it.
The streets were seldom swept. If there was anything to be done, no man exactly knew who was the
person to do it. If anything unpleasant happened,
the blame was sure to light upon half-a-dozen wrong
shoulders before settling on the right ones; and,
when once it got *there*, it did not sit very heavily.
Nobody had the faintest ghost of a notion as to what
became of the public moneys that were levied of a
quarter-day by means of rates: and those who spent
these funds had less notion than the rest. Finally,
no Government employé had ever been seen to do
any other work there than draw his salary. In fact
it was a well-governed town.

And how could it have been otherwise, when
one considered the number of Government functionaries which Touscrétins, in common with most
other French towns, then as now, possessed? They
were innumerable, unimaginable, ensconced everywhere; roosting on every perch, lodged in every con-

ceivable nook; very rats in number, cohesiveness, and rodent appetite. Perhaps I may as well give a list of them:—A prefect, a secretary-general, and three councillors of prefecture; a president of the tribunal, four assistant-judges, a stipendiary justice of the peace, two clerks of court, and a public prosecutor; a receiver-general of taxes and two sub-receivers; a verificator of weights and measures, a chief of the custom-house, and two lieutenants; a high-keeper of the woods and forests (there were none to keep), and two sub-keepers; a commissary of police and a deputy commissary; a captain of gendarmerie and his lieutenant; a rector of academy, a postmaster, a keeper of the archives (which consisted of one deal box full of papers), and two sub-keepers; a chief engineer, an inspector of roads and bridges, and four assistant engineers; a bishop, two vicars-general, one dean, one archdeacon, six canons, two rectors, and eleven curates: tailing upon which gallant procession was an army of five hundred and thirty-seven clerks, postmen, wood-rangers, custom-house officers, tax-gatherers, gendarmes, beadles, vergers, policemen, inspectors of quartpots and firlots, tipstaff court ushers, prison jailers, prison governors, and police spies—all of whom, without exception, were remunerated out of the public purse. Taking the thing in the aggregate, the cost of the

town of Touscrétins to the State (Touscrétins, exclusive of its functionaries and their families, boasted
a population of five thousand and three souls), was
about three million five hundred thousand francs,
or, say, £150,000 a year. What Touscrétins gave
back to the State in exchange for these sums,
neither I nor anybody else have ever been able to
determine.

Now it is easy to comprehend the sort of dismay
that fell upon everybody when it was heard one
morning that a stranger had come within the town,
who felt disposed to criticize this state of things. It
is never pleasant to be criticized. When a man has
a good-sized wen that has taken up its abode on the
nape of his neck, he does not thank you for calling
attention to this wen; holding it up to scorn, and
proposing violently to cut it off. So it is with a
town that has a nice little cluster of abuses flourishing somewhere about it. Much better let the wen
and the abuses alone, says Worldly Wisdom, and so
said they of Touscrétins. They would have spoken
outright on the subject to the greatest man in the
world, had he attempted to reform them; but their
sentiments found much more indignant expression
upon their discovery that their new-come critic was
not any mighty statesman or bishop from Paris—no
grandee traveller or sage from the other side of the

Pyrenées—but simply that lanky young bit of an engineer from the Polytechnic School, who had not been in the town six days.

Somehow the news of this scandal reached the prefecture, and did not much surprise me, for I had guessed from the expression of young Torreau's eyes, and a certain look of being constantly ready to argue the point with you, that he would be an Ishmael, finding few to agree with him. But the intelligence amazed and disconcerted my chief, the Prefect; the fact being, that M. de Feucontenu was a sort of reformer himself, and, like a good many of that kind, naturally looked upon every other reformer as a trespasser upon his own reserved ground. Not that M. de Feucontenu, mind, went in for reform in the sense of improvement—that, of course, would have been going a little too far for a prefect. But, for instance, if he found that a thing had long been done *this* way, it was odds but he suggested one should try and do it *that* way, just for a change; and if everything went wrong from being done *that* way—as it sometimes did—the public were fain to own that M. le Préfet had paid his tribute to the modern idea of progress by his spirited attempt at innovation. It is almost needless to add that M. de Feucontenu was comparatively young—not more than five and forty—and expected to earn promotion by his indefatigable energy. The prefectorate of Touscrétins was his first high post, and being his secretary, it was I who penned the remarkable despatches to the Home Office, in which he recapitulated his "reforms," and stated his object, which was to convince the population that Government had an eye unceasingly and vigilantly fixed upon all their needs. When, therefore, M. de Feucontenu came by the knowledge of what young Torreau was up to, he frowned and exclaimed: "This young fellow is making a bad beginning; it seems he has several times uttered opinions that were most bold to listen to. I should have thought better of a man of his education."

"And not yet twenty-five," ejaculated Mdme. de Feucontenu, as who should say—"So young and so depraved!"

"Have you any precise information, sir, as to what Torreau has been saying or doing?" I inquired, for I had as yet heard no specific charge adduced.

"Well," said M. de Feucontenu, with a rather scared expression, "I hear that, on his very first day, he remarked that five engineers were being employed to do what could very well be accomplished by a single one; also that there were twice too many workmen; but—what is infinitely graver than this— he went the length of complaining of the works themselves, said that the road was unskilfully planned, that it might have been cut at half the cost, and have been at once more convenient and more durable. You understand the effect this produced upon M. Nul. For a man of talent to be criticized by one of his own subordinates is a most painful situation, especially when there seems a likelihood of public opinion agreeing with the subordinate."

"Is there a likelihood of that?" asked Raoul de Gardefer, laughing.

"Public opinion always goes wrong," answered M. de Feucontenu. "Don't you think, Blamont, you had better go and call upon this young fellow, and you too, Gardefer? Point out to him what a mistaken course he is following; explain that what carping minds call abuses are in most instances the vital elements of certain systems of government, which it is the interest, nay, the duty, of all order-loving persons to uphold. Add, moreover, that for a young functionary to display too much zeal is not seemly, being an implied slight on the capacity of his superiors. In fact, talk him over, turn his mind towards suitable subjects, and try to make him a little more like yourselves."

"I don't know whether we are to accept that as a compliment," laughed the Lieutenant, as he shook hands with Mdme. la Préfête, and buckled on his sword.

"To-night is my *Thé-Dansant*," smiled the Préfête; "you will do well to bring M. Torreau back with you."

III.

Mdme. la Préfête's Dancing Teas were generally well thronged, and when Raoul de Gardefer and I entered the rooms towards ten, bringing young Torreau with us in tow, they were more than half filled with the cream of that society skimmed off the top of our population of five thousand and three souls. I cannot say young Torreau had shown himself much overwhelmed with the sense of the honour done him by his invitation to the tea. He even seemed to regret the four francs he was compelled to disburse on a pair of white gloves, and made no secret of his reluctance to introduce himself into an extremely tight pair of patent-leather boots. But there he was, notwithstanding, dressed like everybody, and surveying the contortionate scene of a prefectoral hop, with the smileless face and the serious gaze of a man who has some sort of idea that he is being hoaxed, and would like to know what possible pleasure human beings can find in jumping about in this

way. We introduced him to the mistress of
house, who was still young, and pretty, and ver
fable, and asked him whether he danced. '
no!" said he, in the same tone as if the mutt
corollary were, "not I." "But I will find y(
partner," continued she, laughing a little. "We:
you do, Madame," was his quiet answer, "we
both be falling down together over those slip
boards, and there will be somebody's leg broker

This was the sort of thing that Raoul de Gar(
and I had been undergoing during the whole a
noon. Young Torreau had not been influence
the faintest degree by our visit of remonstra
On the contrary, he had beguiled us into
troversy, and, bringing the heavy artillery of lo
syllogisms to bear on every proposition we
vanced, routed us hip and thigh, the pair o
On walking into his rooms on the topmost fla
the "Lion d'Or," we had found him covering
enormous sheet of foolscap with respectful obse
tions addressed to the Minister of Public Works.
the first place, he requested to be sent to s
other town, for, as there were already three i
engineers than there was any necessity for,
looked upon himself as a useless incumbrance.
the next place, he submitted that if every (
road were cut on the same extravagant plan as

one which he had seen, and with the same total disregard of scientific principles, there was no need to pay engineers for doing such work—it might just as well be intrusted to navvies or stonebreakers. He concluded by offering to complete the road himself at a third of the present expense if he were allowed to do so untrammelled, that is, without the assistance of his chief, M. Nul, whom he regarded as a most incapable individual.

"Well, but," exclaimed Raoul de Gardefer aghast, and yet scarcely able to keep from laughing, as young Torreau coolly read us this document, "you surely don't mean to say that you intend sending that?"

"Why not?" asked Jules Torreau, turning round on his chair, and nibbling the end of his pen-holder. Through the glasses of his spectacles gleamed that expression of being ready to argue which I had instinctively learned to look upon as hopeless.

"I mean you can hardly think of ramming your head so completely into a hornets' nest," pursued the Lieutenant.

"I don't see that," protested Jules Torreau. "Who are the hornets?"

Raoul de Gardefer explained in an easy way that every Government office was a nest of hornets for those who went there to call attention to abuses.

Perhaps if the abuse was a very, very small one, and the person thriving upon it a very, very small person, there was a remote prospect of the abuse receiving the most attentive consideration of a very, very small clerk, bearing a personal grudge against the very small person; and perhaps the abuse would be removed to this extent, that the very small person would be dismissed, and replaced by a cousin or nephew of the very small clerk, who would lose no time in implanting some other abuse worse than that which had been eradicated. But for any man, not a sworn foe to his own peace, to presume attacking abuses fostered by people holding a certain status, eminent, or wealthy, or distantly connected with one or more clerks paid handsomely for doing nothing at the public cost, was about as promising a way of spending one's time as the trying to stop a mountain torrent with the bottom of one's wig, or the riding full tilt at a stone wall, or the going to do battle with a hippopotamus, armed with a wooden paper-cutter.

"Ah! but these are no mere charges," exclaimed young Torreau, bridling up. "I can prove them—prove everything. See here," and he caught up an imposing sheet, illustrated with diagrams, geometrical figures, and exhaustive foot-notes. "Here is the plan of the road such as I would have it, and here is Nul's plan. Mine, you see, saves half-an-hour's walk between this point and that. It also takes one under shelter of a stretch of rocks, which would prevent the road being continually swept by winds, and, in the event of war—should we ever be invaded from the South—would offer a sure line of march to our troops and enable them to entrench themselves as if in a fortress. Nul's road runs along a bleak bit of table-land, where the dust would blind one in summer, and the gales carry one off one's legs in winter. It would be utterly impracticable for military purposes. The expense of keeping it in repair would be terrific, and the only possible way that I can see of maintaining it permanently would be by planting along it a four-league-long avenue of fir-trees, which would cost you may guess what, and not be available for another twenty years."

"Well, you may be right," answered Raoul de Gardefer, surveying the plans not without interest; "but believe me, M. Torreau, the less we youngsters show our elders that their heads are growing soft, the better they will like it; and the less risk we shall run of being op-pressed, re-pressed, and, finally, sup-pressed."

Jules Torreau took back his diagrams, nursed his knee for a few moments, during which he eyed

us both with some little dejection, and at length exclaimed, "If it be so, more's the pity; but I really
see no reason in it for not doing one's duty. If I
notice that a blunder is going to be committed, I
am obviously bound to try and prevent it. I am
sure, Monsieur, that, if you detected any abuses in
your regiment, you would feel it your duty to denounce them."

"God forbid!" exclaimed the Lieutenant, piously.
"I should be writing despatches day and night."

And here the matter ended. Not ended in so
far as talk was concerned, for we talked during
many hours, endeavouring to instil prudence into
our new friend's head. But, talk as we might, we
could never rid him of the conviction that the
official world was a free hunting-ground, where any
one who espied an abuse had a right to aim at it
with loaded barrels, and bring it down if he could.
Impossible to make him understand by a reference
to the game-laws, the harmonious system of pre-
served lands, privileged shooters, and the rest of it.
Impossible to make him grasp the idea, that what
on the part of one man was lawful, coming from
another was poaching. He remained obtuse on this
point; and was just as far wrong as ever when, in
the evening, baffled and worn out by his calm,

quiet obstinacy, we took him to Mdme. la Préfète's party.

"I wonder whether our hostess will be more fortunate with him?" said Gardefer, amused, as the seductive Préfète, after her futile attempt to make young Torreau dance, begged him to lead her to a seat, and tried to draw some conversation out of him.

In a few minutes more we saw the pretty Mdme. de Feucontenu fanning herself and listening, while Jules Torreau, with his hands twitching at his gloves and his patent-leather boots evidently causing him uneasiness, was holding forth with a collected sort of fluency on topics which we could not catch for the braying of a brass band, to the inspiriting strains of which four-and-twenty couples of Touscrétinians were actively quadrilling. It then occurred to me that, under present circumstances, an entertaining person to see would be Jules Torreau's victim, the unhappy M. Nul, whose life had hitherto been devoid of cares. So I cast about for that official until I found him in the card-room, playing whist with the President of the Tribunal, a dowager, and a dummy, and having the air of a man whose whole soul is impendent upon the ace of spades. And yet M. Nul had formerly been one of the most brilliant men of his day, and even now he carried a head that might have sat worthily on the shoulders of Olympian Jupiter. Unfortunately, there was nothing inside the head. It was like a plaster-of-paris bust—brainless; or, to employ a more homely simile, it resembled one of those walnuts which are, indeed, large and robust-looking without, but which inside have nought but the ghostly vestige of a kernel. M. Nul had begun in the same way as young Torreau —by the Polytechnic School. Like his subaltern, he had come out thence at the top of the list, with spectacles and a brain-fever; but, unlike him, the brain-fever seemed never to have left his head, but to have settled there under the chronic form of a mild imbecility, harmless to himself personally, but fatal to every species of work which he undertook. Of course, however, nobody amongst the public noticed that M. Nul was imbecile, nor that his work was trash; for it is one of the happiest effects of the competitive examination mania prevalent in this age that a youth who, by dint of stupendous cramming, manages to distance a certain number of other youths at twenty, is held to be wise, and an object meet for distinction ever after; and this though every particle of the knowledge acquired in his laborious cram may have leaked out of his pate, like water through a sieve, long before he has attained the ripe age of twenty years and six weeks.

So M. Nul on starting in his professional career was loaded with favours. He made roads which crumbled away, and built bridges that fell in, and water-dykes which burst, and aqueducts that flooded whole miles of country; and, thanks to a long series of such works, waxed each year higher in public esteem, until he had reached his present post, that of chief engineer of an entire department, where he did an incredible deal of harm in an innocent way, and was universally respected. So much respected that, in the hour of danger, not a man but would have put his whole confidence in M. Nul, and been brought to grief by him, with faith unshaken in his merits. Alas! what am I saying? The hour of danger *did* come, and, not one department only, but our whole country put its faith in M. Nul. For were they not all Messieurs Nul, those princes, generals, strategists, lawyers, who in the hour of France's need were in charge of the helm, and in one short year steered her out of the sea of glory, where she had so long and so proudly sailed, on to the rocks and shoals where her greatness and fame have been wrecked? But, after all, why talk of this? It is a thing of the past now—and words mend nothing.

M. Nul finished his game as I was watching him, counted his cards carefully twice over and ejaculated—

"I have one trick."

Which trick being the one needed to win the rubber, M. Nul slowly pocketed the stakes, rose with equal slowness from the table, and took up his position in a doorway, doing nothing and saying nothing. I approached him and wished him good evening; and then I observed that his eyes were turned with something of an uneasy expression towards the corner of the adjoining room, where young Jules Torreau was still discoursing with Madame la Préfète. It was not difficult to perceive that, placid as M. Nul might be, the advent of young Jules had introduced an element of bitterness into his hitherto vapid existence, though probably he did not quite understand what this bitterness was, nor what it meant.

"I have been calling to-day upon your new assistant M. Torreau," I remarked, half experimentally.

"Yes, Torreau. His name's Torreau. Jules Torreau is the new engineer's name. I am making a road, and he says he could make a road. But mine's better." M. Nul turned his opinion over once or twice in his mind as if to give his rival every chance, and then repeated with great satisfaction, "Mine's better."

"And after you have completed the road, I believe you are to begin a new reservoir?"

16*

"Yes, a reservoir; a new reservoir. A new reservoir is what we are going to begin. And it will be a good reservoir." Again M. Nul turned over this sentiment once or twice in order that his rival might have the fairest play, and repeated with increased satisfaction, "It will be a good reservoir."

Just at this moment M. de Feucontenu, the Prefect, came hurrying along through the ball-room, upset, and holding a newspaper in his hand.

"Ah," said he, catching sight of us, "look at this, M. Nul, and you, Blamont. Here are pretty goings on. This is last night's *Gazette des Boulevards* just come from Paris, and it contains the first of a series of articles headed LETTRES D'UN FONCTIONNAIRE, which is nothing but a pasquinade upon this town and everybody connected with it. Just see this: it describes our town to the life; and this—a 'prefect whose brains are like the froth on the top of a pint-pot,' that must be me; and here again—an 'engineer who is an ass,' that can only be you. By heavens! there is but one man who can have written this, and it must be that young Torreau; certain engineering terms that he has let slip in betray him. Egad! he must have set to work upon us the very morning after he got here. And to think that we are promised three of these letters every week *until all abuses shall have been divulged!*"

In blank dismay the prefect handed the paper to M. Nul and reiterated, "Three letters every week!"

M. Nul took the journal, turned it over and said profoundly: "*La Gazette des Boulevards. La Gazette des Boulevards* is the name of this paper. And he says, 'an engineer who is an ass.' Yes, certainly, that can only be me."

We were here joined by l'Abbé Pincette, chaplain of the prefecture, a neat dapper man, who exclaimed, much discontented: "I have been talking with that new engineer, M. Torreau, and I much fear that his mind is not godly. In the first five minutes he told me that the early fathers were sophists, steeped up to the neck in ignorance, and of extremely bad faith in controversy. Also, that he declined to believe Christianity was the orgin of civilization, but that he was ready to argue the point."

"And he was just as bad in what he said to me," chimed in Mdme. la Préfète, arriving with flushes of ill-concealed indignation on her pretty face. "I asked him whether he thought he should like our town, and he answered that perhaps he might if it were rebuilt and the inhabitants changed. Then I was telling him about the burning of the prefecture forty years ago, and he said it must have inconvenienced me greatly, just as if I was alive at that time and already Préfète."

After this, it stood evident that it was all up with Jules Torreau. Abandoned by Church, State, and womankind together, he was on the down-road to perdition by the express, and with all brakes up.

But I am afraid I should weary you if I were to recapitulate *seriatim* all the episodes of young Torreau's Odyssey in the town of Touscrétins. If you have ever watched the career of a dog suspected of madness through the streets of an alarmed city, you must have observed how the hue-and-cry is first raised by some girl with a broomstick, then caught up by some ostler with a bucket, and how the inhabitants on both sides of the road, terrified by the sounds, issue out of their houses—when the dog is past—armed with sticks, old matchlocks, pitchforks, and join in the chase, howling frenziedly and at almost as great a rate as the dog himself. So it was with young Torreau. To all intents and purposes he was, in the eyes of Touscrétins, a mad dog; and when it was an ascertained fact that he both barked and bit, the population showed him no quarter. All those noble creatures called Vested Interests were up and after him at full cry. Every man who drew a sixpence from the State coffers, or wished to draw sixpence, or had a cousin desiring to draw sixpence, shrieked and raved. "For a man, himself a functionary, to lay bare the sores of his profession, to hold up abuses to the public eye, to clamour for their cure—Horror! Grief! Scandal!" Unluckily for young Torreau, he had spared nobody. In those letters to the Paris newspaper, he laid about him with the undiscriminating energy and the entire impartiality of youth. His blows fell with terrific thwacks to the right and left of him, upon necks and shoulders, heads and tails. Not a man holding office but had a weal to show; not one but had been excoriated in some tender place by this diabolical and incisive operator. Voted an unmitigated nuisance by the whole official community, he was taxed with the authorship of the letters, and denied them. But this would not do. The letters had attracted notice; they were making the Parisians laugh; the Government were surprised and indignant at them. As for the inhabitants of Touscrétins, they congregated round the diligence when it came in with the papers from Paris, and grabbed excitedly at the numbers, to see who was the new victim. Under these circumstances, M. de Feucontenu, in the interests of order and morality, felt it binding upon him to take a resolution. To the three hundred and odd postmasters of his department he issued orders that they would examine all parcels "of a suspicious appearance" destined for Paris—that is, all parcels that looked as if they might contain copy.

By these means young Torreau's guilt was clearly traced home to him. His signature was there, at the bottom of a letter to the editor. Here was a case of *flagrans delictum.* It was determined to make an example of him.

I should mention cursorily that throughout all the storm of obloquy that raged over young Torreau's misguided head, and throughout all the persecutions that were eventually levelled at him — persecutions in which M. de Feucontenu, my chief, took the leading part, egging on the inert M. Nul, who, certainly, had not originality enough of his own left to persecute anybody—throughout all this troublous time, I say, there were two of us who stuck faithfully by young Torreau, and those two were Raoul de Gardefer and myself. We stuck by him because we had got to like him. We had little fellow-feeling for the knight-errant crusades he had undertaken, like Cervantes' great hero, against social wind-mills. Indeed, I, for my part, enter my most distinct protest against any man on this snug earth of ours attempting to reform anything. When I see an abuse flourishing anywhere, I am for having it let alone, until it dies a natural and venerable death; for a long experience has convinced me that as fast as one abuse disappears another springs up in its place, and that—to use the words of a clever Frenchman—"*Plus ça*

change et plus c'est la même chose." But
young Torreau, because of his earnestness
cause he was a good fellow. When one
stalk in his black clothes through the sc
ways of Touscrétins, with his hands bui
hind pockets, his eyes fixed on the pave
his head evidently cogitating over some
for his next philippic, it was impossible 1
that here was a fanatic who might be v
who, in taking up the cudgels against Sc
clearly following the road which Nature h.
out for him beforehand as if with a piece
Then, he was generous: his parsimony onl
to himself. On his own needs he sper
nothing; but if asked to subscribe to the
pleasures of others, he gave handsome
prodigally. Moreover, he was plucky witl
tation. Being dragged into a quarrel—
one of his letters—by an irate individual
chosen to consider himself alluded to, he
out and stood his adversary's fire; then,
own turn came to aim, he had said, "
worth killing!" and discharged his pistol

So when we perceived that official
was weaving its net round him and d
meshes every day closer, we resolved to
more attempt to expostulate with him and

It was not our second attempt, nor yet our tenth, for we had amicably bantered and cautioned him whenever thrown in his company. But banter he did not understand, and caution was lost upon him. It was only by elasticity of hope that we could expect that he would see his danger more accurately this time, and that we should be more fortunate. We accordingly bent our steps towards the "Lion d'Or."

But we had been forestalled, and by the persons best qualified to pull him out of his pit, if so be that he could be pulled out. When we knocked at his door, we found him surrounded by the whole Torreau family in tears: Torreau senior mopping his face with his handkerchief and holding his hat dismally between his knees; Mdme. Torreau with her bonnet-strings unfastened and her maternal bosom heaving, whilst her hands grasped one of young Jules's with a sort of entreaty; pretty Mdlle. Victorine Torreau with her eyes red; and, on various chairs about the room, the uncle in the tailoring way, the other uncle who sold the simili-panamas, and a ripe cluster of maiden aunts. All these worthy people having somehow heard that the hope and pride of their little circle had got himself into hot water, but not knowing, nor able to guess, how that could be, had hurried down in a tremor of anxiety, but with the vague belief that their presence would set everything to rights. They were now adjuring young Jules not to cause them grief and trouble—not to disappoint their long and fondly cherished hopes of seeing him great and prosperous.

"But really, mother," young Jules was exclaiming, half-impatiently, as Raoul and I crossed the threshold, "one would think I had been committing some great crime to hear the way you talk."

"Oh, gentlemen," said Mdme. Torreau, after we had been formally introduced, "you must excuse these tears; but we have been so overcome. Our only son, and never given us a day's uneasiness till now!"

"I wouldn't believe it at first," ejaculated Torreau senior, sadly. "Wouldn't believe that Jules had taken to writing in newspapers."

"And against the Government!" continued Mdme. Torreau.

"Against the Government!" echoed Torreau senior; and in a doleful way he took up some papers lying open on young Jules's desk, and read them for the twentieth time. It seems that one of them was the official reply to that memorable despatch in which young Jules, not yet in his place a week, had stated his candid opinion of his chief, M. Nul; and the others were categorical demands on the part of Government to be told whether or no

M. Torreau was the author of certain letters reflecting disparagingly on divers eminent persons and institutions? It turned out that young Jules had given as his final answer that he refused to afford any explanation whatever on this question, which he contended that nobody had any right to put to him. And conformably to his practice, he had argued this last point.

"I am afraid all this will end badly," was Torreau senior's desponding commentary, whereat Mdme. Torreau began to weep anew.

"Oh, my child," pleaded she, "do you not remember, when you won the Great Prize, how I cried for joy; and how, when the people applauded you, I felt so proud and grateful that I could have gone down on my knees and thanked God before everybody for what He was doing for us? And do you not remember how, when we came down the great staircase amidst all your schoolfellows cheering us, my arm trembled on yours, and I whispered in your ear that, heaven willing, you should always stand as high in the esteem of your friends as you did then? Dear child, do not let the dreams we then made for you come to nothing. You are our only hope, darling; you will have pity on our old age, won't you?" And the good lady threw her arms, sobbing, round her son's neck.

"You hear what your mother says, Jules," faltered honest Torreau senior, who was himself fairly upset; and, indeed, I think at that moment there were not many dry eyes in the room.

"Come, Torreau," said Raoul de Gardefer, who had been twitching very nervously at his moustache during all this, "we will turn over a new leaf, won't we? This sort of thing doesn't do at our age, old fellow—it really doesn't."

"God bless you, sir!" ejaculated a maiden aunt.

Young Jules was sustaining his mother and kissing her. He was extremely pale; but what his answer would have been none of us ever knew, for at this juncture Mdlle. Jeannine, the maid, having knocked, entered with a large letter, in a blue envelope, and with a Government seal, which she presented to young Jules.

Then a great silence fell upon everybody, and there also fell, I imagine, a presentiment of evil. We all fixed our eyes apprehensively on the letter. The only cool person in the room was young Jules, who broke the seal.

This is what he read:—

" *Ministry of Public Works, Paris.*

"Sir,—I have the honour to inform you that your answers to my despatch of the 21st being pre-eminently unsatisfactory, and your public career, though short, having been marked from the first by an habitual disregard of duty, a flagrant spirit of insubordination, and by the authorship of certain newspaper articles, rendered the more culpable from your persistency in denying them, I have arrived at the conclusion submitted to me by M. Nul, your chief, and by M. de Feucontenu, the Prefect of Touscrétins, that you are not fitted for the post with which the Government had entrusted you. I have, therefore, recommended to the Minister of War that your commission should be cancelled, and you cease from this day to be a public servant.

"I have the honour to remain, sir,

"Your most obedient servant,

"CASIMIR BARBOTTE,

"*Minister of Public Works.*"

One might have heard a fly buzz in the room when Jules Torreau, after reading this dismissal, threw it down upon the table. The melancholy pause was broken by Mdme. Torreau, who dried her eyes and said, "My child, your sister and I will go and throw ourselves at the Emperor's feet, and ask him to forgive you."

IV.

But young Jules was definitively overboard, and no mother's tears or supplications could avail to reinstate him. We lost sight of him. Like a meteor, he had flashed for a brief space over our benighted town of Touscrétins, and like a meteor he disappeared, leaving behind him for a while a luminous trail in the shape of many grudges glowing in the breasts of such personages as he had frightened. But by-and-by, for want of further causes of resentment to feed them, these grudges flickered out. Men are too busy nowadays to hate long—our passions, like our affairs, go railway pace. So Jules was forgotten, and few amongst his former friends or foes knew, or cared to know, that the caustic writer who began about that time to take a lead in the opposition press, under the pseudonym of Maillotin, and whose articles grew daily more vigorous, more violent, and—must one add it?—more unreasonable, was the same as the young engineer who had broken his first lances by tilting at M. Nul. I, for my part, had let the fact almost slip from my memory, so true it is that friends to keep in mind must keep in sight, when I was put in remembrance of it by being unexpectedly brought into contact with my old acquaintance, in the spring of the present twelve-month, 1871.

Some six or seven years had elapsed since our last meeting, and our poor France was woefully altered. But events had wrought in her greater changes than time. The Second Empire, and its abuses, had been swept away, and we were now living under the Commune de Paris, which was to do away altogether with abuses, or import new ones of its own, people were not yet quite clear which. Of the persons present at that family scene in the garret of the "Lion d'Or," two at least were in their graves—the excellent M. and Mdme. Torreau, who, I fancy, owed their ends to something subtler than the ailments which human doctors can cure. Mdlle. Victorine had been married by her brother, not to a husband who, like herself, had "cent mille livres de dot," but to Celestin Joubarbe, her father's ex-apprentice, who had not got a penny. Raoul de Gardefer become a colonel, war and valour aiding, was besieging the capital with the Versailles troops, and I—but never mind about myself. Suffice it to say that I was in Paris, and not quite certain whether my opinions were likely to secure me a long enjoyment of freedom under the peculiar kind of liberty we were inaugurating.

It was a lovely April morning, the sky so blue and speckless, the sun so golden, the breath of the air so balmy, that everything seemed possible in such weather—everything but civil strife, which struck one as a sacrilege. The streets were alive and gay with colours; battalions trooping with their scarlet facings, blue képis, and flashing bayonets. Artillery lumbering gaily over the paving-stones, with the men seated by threes on the gun-carriages, smoking and shouting to one another. Along the roads

workmen arm-in-arm, and six in a line, with cartri
boxes round their waists and rifles slung over
shoulders, singing and cheering when a batt:
passed, or waving their caps when some comm
chieftain, not over firmly seated on his cha
cantered by smiling, and doing his best to look
he were not holding on by the pommel. Mo:
the shops closed. On the walls large and be
fully printed white proclamations, headed, "R
blique Française—Commune de Paris." And
side them red ones, more shabbily printed an
suing from the Comité Central of the National Gu
From the roof of one house in every twenty,
from five windows out of a hundred, fluttered l:
the crimson banner of the Insurrection—a das
standard enough if it had not signified fire
carnage—and over the church doors, now cle
beamed the words, "Liberté, Égalité, Fratern
As a grim and ironical commentary to these mot
cannon booming faintly in the distance, and ar
lance-waggons passing every now and then thro
the streets slowly, and loaded with wounded.

"I should do much better not to go out,"
my friends, as I was putting on my hat; but fric
always speak in this strain, and after walking a'
for an hour unmolested, I was reflecting how
tremely wise I had been not to follow their ad

Just then I was in the Place Vendôme, having been taking a look at the column which my morning paper had informed me was doomed, and emerging into the Rue Castiglione, was about to cross the road, when the clatter of hoofs became audible, and a goodly cavalcade burst in sight. It turned out to be the Citoyen Quelque-chose, member of the Commune, and Generalissimo of something, riding somewhere, in gaudy apparel, accompanied by his morganatic spouse and a brilliant staff. Of course, the central figure of the picture was the morganatic spouse. She was riding a handsome charger— a white one—probably requisitioned from the ex-imperial stables, and cut as brave a figure as could be wished in her blue habit, silver-laced jacket, and white fur busby with red egret. As the whole procession filed past at an amble, she heading it by a neck, she gave a little toss of her comely head, and slightly lowered her eyes on me, evidently expecting to be bowed to. I lifted my hat with pleasure, musing as I did so, that if the Commune de Paris did nothing worse than dress up pretty women in fancy costume, there was no very great objection to be taken against it. But when it came to be a question of saluting the tag-rag and bobtail staff, who jolted behind like so many sacks perched on saddles, and answering their cries of " *Vive la*

Commune!" I thought my philosophy had gone far enough, and I walked on with my hat on my head and my tongue silent.

"Hullo there!" shouted a workman behind me, who had been a spectator of the whole incident and was scandalized, "just you stop; you never cried *' Vive la Commune!'*"

"No, I really did not," was my answer.

"Then just do so," said he with a beery hiccough, and laying his hand on my sleeve.

I shook myself free.

"Suppose you mind your own business, citizen."

"Mind my own business!" he yelped. "I like that. Hi! citizens, here's a traitor, a Versaillais, an agent of Bismarck's! He cries, 'Down with the Republic!'"

In a trice I was surrounded. At the most peaceful times it requires but a few seconds to collect a Parisian mob, but in times of war or rebellion the mobs seem to spring from the pavement ready made and ready raving.

"A Versaillais! a traitor! to prison with him!" was the cry; and I was immediately apprehended, jostled, and pushed forward, a squad of street-boys protesting energetically against the waste of time involved in the conveyal of me to prison, and sug-

17*

gesting that I should be shot there and then as a wholesome warning.

Now this may be amusing enough to write about at three months' distance, but it was not particularly funny then; and I began to perceive, as my captors hurried me along with more haste than ceremony, that I had got myself into an awkward predicament. It was then, that raising my eyes by a providential chance, they lit upon a placard on which were the names of all the members of the Commune, and conspicuous amongst those names, that of Jules Maillotin. "Surely," thought I, "this Maillotin must be the same as my old friend Jules Torreau;" and without pausing to meditate whether my old friend would prove to be still as fraternally disposed towards me as I was towards him,—for it is not only princes who turn cold shoulders on old but inconvenient acquaintances—I cried in a firm voice: "Citizens, I demand to be taken before the Citizen Maillotin." "If Torreau's memory be short," murmured I to myself, "I shall probably be shot; but nothing venture nothing have."

The beery citizen, who was clutching tight hold of me by the neck-cloth, as much I fancy to steady himself as to drag me, stopped and said: "You know the Citizen Maillotin?"

"He knows the Citizen Maillotin!" echoed another

citizen behind, who had been tranquilly exploring my pockets.

An enthusiastic female Republican had rid me of my handkerchief, and tied it round her neck. She threw it back to me, and said: "If you are a friend of Maillotin's they won't harm you; if you're not—*cou-ic!*" and with a forefinger she made a graceful gesture of passing a knife across her throat.

"We'll take him to the Hôtel-de-Ville," chorused all the citizens together; and to the Hôtel-de-Ville we went.

I need not, I think, stop to describe this interesting edifice, which has since been offered up as a sacrifice to the genius of democracy; but I would remark that those who missed seeing the Hôtel-de-Ville whilst it was in possession of the Commune, have lost something for which no sight either in this or the next generation is likely to compensate them. It was pleasant and unique—a thing to see if only to acquire an idea of the manner in which human nature will disport itself when allowed to go its own ways. There were no doubt curious things to be seen at the Hôtel-de-Ville in '48 and '93. But on both of those former auspicious occasions, when the world was turned upside down, there was some sort of cohesion, some discipline, some order amidst the general hash, which kept matters going with an ap-

pearance of ship-shape. Nothing of that sort however this time. Here we had the genuine article—
democracy pure, each man his own king, and declin-
ing to render obedience to anybody or anything
under any pretext whatever. To tell the truth, I
think when we begin to accept democracy, we had
better go the whole length at once; there is something logical and elevating in the position which
seduces one. In the first courtyard, going in, I heard
a captain call to one of his men, and say it was
time for him to come and mount guard; and the man
answered that he would come presently, when he
had finished his game of picquet. In a vestibule
another captain was giving himself a brush-down,
whilst half his company lolled around him on the
floor in easy attitudes, and apparently much amused
to see the efforts their chief was making to reach a
particular speck of mud situated in the small of his
back, and not attainable by the brush. On the grand
staircase, resplendent with marble and gilt bronze, I
was much pleased to see a frugal housewife seated
and shelling haricot-beans into a basin. Of course,
she would have been much more comfortable shelling her beans at home, and probably felt it; but then
this would not have been Republican. The moment
you have free institutions, the Municipal Palace
evidently becomes the proper place to shell beans in.

"We want the Citizen Maillotin," hiccoughed my beery captor for the twentieth time, as we trudged all together into the State apartments.

"You'll find him in one of the rooms somewhere," answered a citizen in a blouse, who was scratching his name with a pin on one of M. Baudry's mural paintings.

"There—through that door," bawled another, recumbent on a rosewood table: "I saw him go in an hour ago," and in another moment I was standing in a sumptuous chamber, which I remembered as a supper-room when Prefect Haussmann was still reigning and gave those famous balls of his. At a table, which must many a time have groaned under the weight of iced pails of Cliquot, truffled pasties, golden fruit-vases, and other products of a pampered civilization, my old friend Jules Torreau, in a uniform of officer of the National Guard, was seated, writing.

He shaded his eyes with his hand, looked at me a moment, and said, recognizing me, "Ha, Blamont, this is a surprise!"

It was the same smileless face, quick but quiet way, and penetrating expression of the eyes; and it was also the same grasp; for he shook hands with me as he had done on the day when Raoul de

Gardefer and I had accompanied him to the diligence to see him starting on his exile and cheer
him. Perhaps the grasp was even rather warmer and
longer.

"Then you know this individual?" cried the beery
citizen, who, to make some kind of amends for having half-throttled me, began fumbling my shirt-front
with his hands, setting my cravat to rights, and trying to make me look reputable.

"Yes, I know him, and will answer for him under
any circumstances." This Torreau said, without so
much as knowing of what I was accused; but he
reiterated his declaration when my crime was explained to him, and vouched for my being neither
this nor that, nor anything else likely to injure the
Sovereign People.

"Then we'll put it down that nothing has taken
place, Citizen," said the beery Republican, shoving
out a paw for me to shake. "*Vive la Commune!
Vive le Citoyen Maillotin!*"

The cheers were taken up with tremendous
energy by the citizens behind, who repeated them
again and again. They even overdid it, and waxed
prodigal of their own breath. But it was ended at
last, and with one cheer more for everybody in
general not connected with reactionary machinations,

they departed, treading on one another's heels, and leaving me alone with Torreau.

"Well," said I, turning to him, gratefully, "I may consider that I owe you a heavy debt."

"Oh, no," he replied, carelessly: "they would not have hurt you. They are a little rough, but very good fellows, and perfectly honest."

"Yes, honest enough," I answered, noticing, for the first time, that my pocket-book was missing.

"The people have been systematically maligned," continued Torreau. "It has been the interest of those who kept them under foot to paint them as brute beasts; but they are better than their oppressors."

"I hear that you are one of the leading spirits of this movement," I remarked, to change the subject.

"I am but a soldier in a great cause," said he, shortly. There was something of the suppressed exaltation of the fanatic in his tone. "Why do you look at me so gravely?" he added. "You have something you wish to say: you think I am riding with the wrong party?"

I suppose my look must have said more than my tongue, for he took me by the arm, led me towards the window, and, with a rapid gesture in the direction of some National Guardsmen, whom we could see cleaning their rifles in the square below, said, "See, there is a people who have been oppressed and enslaved ever since this country was an inhabited land. Their lot has been to bend the neck, to wallow, and to shed their blood, and that is all. In order that successive dynasties of kings might feast more richly, and carry their heads higher, these poor devils—famished, and beaten, and kept in the brutish belief that their kings were men of different clay to themselves—have fought that ghastly roll of battles which constitutes the history of France during fifteen centuries. One day the people rose and smashed the throne. Its pieces were picked up and nailed together again. They smashed it a second time, with a like result; and again a third. Three times the nation, after breaking its chains, was re-fettered; and now that once more we have broken our shackles, there are men who want to reforge them and bind us anew. But we have had enough of it. France is not to be eternally bandied about, and ridden like a hack-mule by Bonapartes, Bourbons, and Orleanists, one after the other. The people will be their own masters now: work, study, live at peace, and be free. This is what we want, and all we want. What have you to say against us?"

He looked at me hungrily for a reply; but I had no time to give it, for a man with ink on his fingers and a pen in his mouth opened the door, and cried, "Citizen Maillotin, there's to be a sitting of the Commune. Are you coming?"

"Will you accompany me?" asked Torreau, evidently expecting that I was going to refuse. But I accepted. The sittings of the Commune were at that time open to only a very few privileged spectators, among whom no reporters were admitted. Torreau affirmed that he could pass me in, *if I liked*, laying a certain stress upon those words, as if he were not very certain that the proceedings would edify me. But I clung to my resolution; so that, having donned his insignia of office—a brilliant red sash, with a gold fringe, which he girt round his waist — he walked out after the man with the pen, and I followed him.

Along two or three corridors, and through a succession of chambers, all bearing more or less marks of the people's love of quiet work, study, and the rest of it, Torreau and I wended our way till we found ourselves facing the door of the ancient council-room, thronging around which were a number of men with fixed bayonets, who were lamentably unwashed, but who seemed to be acting as a guard of

honour. They let us both through without asking
questions, and in we marched.

Long before reaching the door our ears had been
greeted by the yelping voice of a Citizen, who was
speaking under the effects of strong excitement or
strong alcohol, and this gentleman was still on his
legs when we were admitted to the view of him.
The scene was made up of a long oval table, covered
with a scarlet cloth, and surrounded by fifty-three
scarlet chairs, about two-thirds of which were occupied. On the table, inkstands, pens, and paper for
the use of the few, water-bottles, tumblers, and sugar-
basins for the refreshment of the many. Hanging
on the walls, superb picture-frames bereft of their
canvas—ex-portraits of ex-potentates become exiles.
At one end of the room a monster and, from the
artistic point of view, monstrous statue, of the Republic, by a sculptor name unknown; and behind
this statue, a panoply of crimson flags, with the
rather sinister inscription on a scroll, "GUERRE AUX
TYRANS?" On a row of chairs near the fretted
marble chimney-piece, some half-a-dozen strangers,
brought in, like myself, by members, and sitting
dumb as fish.

Now, I had in my time frequented more than
one popular assembly, and gathered the amusement
that may generally be got out of those places of

entertainment. Especially had I visited what are termed in Paris democratic socialist club debates, and had found enough to laugh at for a whole week after each visit. But this time it was quite another story. What were empty words at the clubs, were words that might be followed by deeds here; for the men who talked held a city of two million inhabitants in their hands, and were free to put into practice all or any of the amusing theories that might pass through their heads. So I took my seat in no great humour for merriment, but chiefly concerned to learn *de visû* who and what the men of the Commune were. I also hoped from my heart of hearts that I might be enabled to change my preconceived opinions respecting some of them; but I cannot say this hope was fulfilled.

The members kept sauntering in every other minute with a leisurely gait, as if they were entering a café. Most of them were in uniforms profusely laced, and one had only to look at their faces for a single moment to gauge the whole worth of the Communal movement, its prospects, and its true signification. There was no Republicanism here— no, not so much as would have filled a nutshell. It was not equality he cared for, that limber workman, who had never worn out a set of tools, and who sat down making great play with his right hand, to show

off an enormous diamond ring which had somehow
got there. Not fraternity that had ever troubled him,
that pale, swaggering, literary Bohemian, grown sour
in writing books which nobody would read, and
starting papers that no one would ever buy; and who
came in, fanning himself ostentatiously with a cam-
bric handkerchief redolent with musk at twenty yards
off. As for liberty, it was not difficult to guess the
definition which those gentlemen would give of that,
the day when liberty began to criticize their little
acts or clash with their little interests. A citizen
whom I had heard of as most hot in favour of press
freedom in the private journalist phase of his existence, proposed, in my hearing, that all newspapers
should be suppressed except those conducted by
members of the Commune, that is, his own and somebody else's, and I should be wrong if I were to state
that this motion was received with any tokens of
disfavour. That there were a very few earnest men
amongst the number nobody will gainsay. Jules
Torreau was earnest, earnest and disinterested; and
he had three or four congenial backers. But I think
when we have said four we shall have gone as far
as truth will allow. As for the rest, I may be mis-
judging them, but can only say that if they were
zealous patriots devoted to their country's good, and
with souls exempt from selfish musings, this did not

show either in their looks or their costume, and least of all in their utterances.

But I must do the Commune this justice—their deliberations were not wordy. The Citizen with the yelping voice spoke about ten minutes, and proved to be less excited than his manner implied; but after him spoke a number of his colleagues, who were content with their hundred words or so a-piece— strange abstemiousness, which first opened my eyes to the expeditious character of debates conducted in the absence of reporters. By the time the tenth spokesman had relieved his mind, most of the members had arrived, and some more spectators with them, so that the room was tolerably full. Amongst the last comers were the Generalissimo whom I had met in the morning, and whom equestrian exercise seemed to have made a little stiff, and his pretty morganatic spouse, who did me the honour of accepting the seat I offered her.

"Allow me to compliment you on your riding, Citoyenne," I remarked, by way of saying something.

"Ah, yes," she answered, with a little pout, "riding is better than stewing here. *On s'embête ici à quarante sous par tête.*"

"Do you ever speak?"

"Sometimes, when they pitch into Alphonse" (Alphonse was the Generalissimo). "He has not got much of a head, Alphonse hasn't; so that when D. or P. or one of those gets jowling with him, he stands no chance unless I get up and take his part. It's against rules, and they cry to me to sit down, but I don't care for that."

"Of course not."

"No. The other day they wouldn't hear me, so I screamed till they did. It was that small fellow there with the grey beard, who had got hold of Alphonse, and was soaping his head for him, because Alphonse had lost two guns in his last sortie. Said I to him, 'If *you'd* had *ten* guns you'd have lost them; and if you'd had twenty you'd have lost *them;* and if you ever get a hundred you'll lose *them;* so there!'"

"And what did he say?"

"He was shut up; there was nothing to answer. Oh, I never stand nonsense, I don't, especially from such as he. Why, he's a dog-clipper; used to cut dog's ears and tails and their hair. There's a trade for a man! When I was in the Quartier Latin, I used to pass him every morning as I went over the Pont des Arts with my work. But there, it's too bad, I declare; they've got hold of Alphonse again.

I say, there, Citizen" (and she rose, extending her small white gloved hand with a riding-whip in it), "I wish you'd let the General alone. Why can't you hit some one else? You had your fling at him last time."

"Will you hold your tongue, Citoyenne?" angrily shouted the member who was presiding—the journalist D., no pleasant man to deal with, silent, gloomy, and cold, a Republican every inch.

"No, I shan't," retorted the Citoyenne, "until the Citizen Faggeaux holds his. What does he tell lies for?"

"Lies!" screamed the Citizen Faggeaux. "I'll prove 'em!"

"This sort of thing is disgraceful," exclaimed Jules Torreau, striking the table with his fist and biting his lips. "Citoyenne," he added, in a tone of voice much sharper and shriller than I should have expected of him, "the next time you interrupt the debates, I shall move that you be forbidden the room. You are not here at the Bal Bullier, but in a National Assembly."

"It was he who began," said the Citoyenne, sulkily, but a little cowed, for Jules Torreau seemed to exercise more prestige than anybody.

"Began or not began, you have no right to open

your mouth," continued Torreau, excitedly; "and as
for you, Citizen Podevin, I think you will feel it your
duty soon to explain to the Commune how you came
by your generalship. In the first hours of the insurrection a great many citizens seem to have created
titles for themselves, and you are probably one of
them. Nothing in your former profession fitted you
for the part you wish to play, and this is no child's
game we are engaged in. You have made three
sorties, and been routed with loss. You have human
lives to account for."

"I'm a general," exclaimed M. Podevin, in alarm
and doggedly. "I will be a general."

"You are always bullying Alphonse," ejaculated
the Citoyenne, with flashing eyes.

"Sit down, Thérèse," mumbled the Generalissimo.

"Well, it comes to this," proceeded Torreau, with
firmness. "If we are to entrust our fate to everybody who thinks himself a soldier, our defence will
last just a fortnight. We cannot help some civilians
becoming generals, for the military men amongst us
are few; but we can take our precautions against incapable men soliciting high posts for the idle grati-
fication of their vanity. I shall, therefore, propose
that every commander who is repulsed or loses guns

shall be tried by court-martial, and, pending the sentence, be kept imprisoned." *

The Citizen Podevin made a most ugly face, and so did a few of his belaced colleagues; but the general sense of the meeting was with Torreau. Seeing this, Torreau stood up and said: "As an engineer I know what resistance can be offered by this fortified city if we are resolute and united and do our duty. But it is not only against incapable generals we have to guard; we must root up that spirit of vanity which is the foundation of every form of weakness and the mainspring of all bad actions. As a nation we have always been too fond of spangled clothes and empty titles: it is for us now, who are republicans, to set the example of self-amendment. I would have a general dress like his soldiers, eat of their food, sleep on the same hard bed as they, and be distinguished from them only by his greater valour and superior learning."

A few of Torreau's friends intimated a grim and hearty assent, but this time the general sense of the meeting did not follow the orator. The citizens who wore embroidered tunics, gold sword-belts, and braided képis, looked at one another and then at their clothes, as though to ask what was the use of

* This law was afterwards passed by the Commune and very stringently executed.

being under a Republic if such clothes and such men were not allowed to air themselves together. And this prevailing opinion found vent on this occasion through the mouth of the Citizen Christophe Bilia, an old acquaintance of mine of club celebrity, who replied with a not dissatisfied glance at his own bright raiment: "Under the Roman Republic, citizen generals did not dress like their soldiers. When they returned home in triumph after victory their costumes were of incomparable richness, and they even stained their faces purple."

"The world has not been marching onward for two thousand years, for us to imitate the mummeries of the ancients," was Torreau's answer, shot back like a dart from a bow. "Besides, you are talking of Rome in her decline. When Rome was a Republic her generals guided the plough like Cincinnatus."

The Citizen Christophe Bilia would have been glad to make a reply, but his classical education had been a little neglected, and he could only exclaim that one should look at a Republican's soul and not his trousers. The discussion was, however, prevented from going further by the entry of a messenger who came in with a despatch from Neuilly and handed it to the President D. This gentleman opened it and read aloud:—

"Neuilly.—The Versailles troops came in great force to the outermost barricade this morning, and after two hours' fighting dislodged us. We lost two hundred killed and wounded and four hundred prisoners, also one mitrailleuse and four field-pieces. The men are much discouraged and complain that we are always left to fight the enemy at unequal odds. We stand in great need of reinforcements.

"THE GENERAL NONPLUSSKI."

There was a moment's silence, and then the President said: "I suppose we had better edit this in the usual way for the public," and he amended the despatch as follows:—

"Neuilly.—The Royalist hordes came in great force to the outermost barricade this morning and were victoriously repulsed after two hours' hard fighting. Their losses are five hundred killed and wounded and seven hundred prisoners, also two mitrailleuses and eight field-pieces. Our own losses are three men slightly wounded. The Royalists are greatly discouraged, but amongst our men the warmest enthusiasm prevails. They routed the enemy to the cry of 'VIVE LA COMMUNE.'

"THE GENERAL NONPLUSSKI."

"Well," said I, as half an hour later I was taking leave of Torreau at the door of the Hôtel-de-Ville, after he had obligingly given me a passport which would guarantee me against further molestation, "I suppose it will be of no more use for me to argue with you now than it used to be seven years ago?"

He shook his head.

"Why argue? justice is on our side. We ask for no more than we have a right to."

"It is not your demands, Torreau, but your way of making them."

"Sword in hand?" and his eye gleamed. "I tell you that nothing was ever wrested from the iron-handed classes but at the sword's point. Then, the opportunity led us on. When, again, should we have a hundred thousand working-men armed? But this is only the beginning. We have been beaten as yet. At our first victory all the great cities in France will rally round us."

"And if the victory should not come?"

"Oh, then—" He turned his eyes full on me, and touching his breast with a slight, simple gesture, said: "I have sacrificed my life beforehand, if that is what you mean."

Honest Torreau! Your motives have been weighed by this time in higher courts than those where human judges sit. You have been arraigned and have pleaded. And surely in that Great Book where the final verdict on men's lives is inscribed, an Arbiter more impartial than we has written: Not Guilty.

V.

The gloomy drama of the Second Siege of Paris
continued—its termination being not hard to foresee,
its incidents becoming daily more interesting to
watch, as the insurgents at bay saw the death circle
growing closer each hour around them, and recognized
that there was no path of escape. I followed with
painful anxiety my friend Torreau's course during
this wretched time, perceived him losing his hold of
the shaggy multitude who had never but in a very
half-hearted way deferred to the guidance of him
and his moderate friends; and I heard of him struggling to the end with a sort of desperation, that the
reins might not altogether slip from his hands. It
was noticed that none of the decrees relating to
executions or demolitions, or arbitrary arrests, bore
his signature. He would have had his revolution be
blameless. He said so, repeated it, found accents
of wildest eloquence in which to adjure his colleagues
not to disgrace the cause for which they were fighting; and, as invariably happens, when men will not
let themselves be carried along by the torrent which

they have let loose, lost his popularity, was accused of being lukewarm, then a traitor, and at last could no longer open his mouth without having the foulest insults flung into his teeth.   I used to see caricatures of him in the Communal comic prints, representing him gibbeted or set in a pillory; that noble organ, the *Père Duchêne*, clamoured that he might be shot; and one day I met him, looking so fagged, careworn, and despondent that, pale as I had always known him in other times, he now seemed but the ghost of his former self.

"You must resign," I said: "the movement has got beyond your control. People must not be able to fix any part of the responsibility of what is being done now, or will be done, on you."

"No," answered he sadly, but resolutely, "I must remain till the catastrophe. I cast in my lot with the movement; I have no right to abandon it in its last hours. Perhaps I may be able to do some good —prevent some evil, I mean; that is the most I can expect now."

I endeavoured to shake his resolution, and alluded, amongst other things, to the hostages, whom the insurgent sheets were threatening every morning with death. He stopped me agitatedly, and exclaimed: "You must not believe that. Oh, great God! no, it would be too horrible. Those men talk worse than they mean. No Frenchman would do that," and he pressed his hand to his forehead.

Almost immediately he added, with some eagerness: "I was able to save two hostages. I got them liberated before it was known to the papers that they had been arrested, else I should never have been able to manage it."

"Who were they?"

He hesitated before replying, and coloured slightly as he did so: "Two old friends, or old foes of mine, who happened to be in Paris: M. de Feucontenu and M. Nul."

This was the last time but one that I saw him. The last time of all was some ten days later, in the closing week of May. The Versailles troops had been in Paris since the Sunday evening, and were already masters of more than half the town. Who that saw it can ever forget that week? The unspeakable horror of the battles in the streets, the resistance, the massacres, and, worse than all, those appalling fires that turned the sky to a blood-red over the distracted city, and made people think that the end of time itself was at hand! The quarter in which I lived was one of the first to be taken. Bullets and shells crashed past our windows, carrying away great fragments of balconies, huge masses of stone, and reducing many houses to a condition of smoking ruins. It was only by a sort of miracle that the particular roof under which I was sheltered was spared; and when I say spared, I simply mean that it was left standing. As to its condition, it looked as if it had stood an entire siege by itself. When I was told that I might at length go out without being taken between two fires, I descended, and found the threshold of our *porte-cochère* covered with a great pool of blood, which the porter's wife was going to wash away with buckets of water and mop; and—ghastly and never-to-be-forgotten sight—three men sitting in a row, cold and stark, propped up by the porter's door, and with great holes in their faces and chests, showing where bullets had struck them. They had been shot in our very yard, for trying to burn the house, and, in fact, the whole street. The porter had then seated them in a row, in order, he said, to act as a warning. Just outside the house a woman stretched out on her face dead. Further on, eleven men in one red heap. At the street corner, corpses in such number that a pile of them had been made on each side of the roadway to allow people room to pass between. The mud in this roadway was purple, and the walls were spattered with blood, as if it had been done with a brush.

I hurried on shuddering and saw a public-house, which was deserted. A bullet had struck the owner, a woman, behind her pewter counter, and she sat with half her lifeless body extended over it and her arms hanging down. In her fall she had upset a copper pitcher of wine, which crimsoned the floor. In this house there was a birdcage with a bullfinch in it. The cage had had no harm, and the bullfinch was blithely singing.

Coming to an open place where four roads met, a dusty sentinel cried to me hoarsely to pass to the left. On the right were the crumbling remnants of a barricade that had held out for six hours, and in front of that barricade, 127 dead bodies, heaped up into a hillock. On the top of this heap was stretched out, stiff and white, a woman in a riding-habit, and with her long silky hair horribly daggled by a wound which had carried half her forehead away. It was the young mistress of the General or Citizen Podevin, whom I had seen in such spirits and beauty a few weeks before, with her mouth wide open and features hideously distorted, as if she had been struck down while crying for mercy; and the Citizen Podevin himself I saw lying dead close to her.

All this was so abominably shocking that I fled forward, looking neither to the right or left of me.

What I wanted was to find Torreau, to offer him a shelter, and keep him hidden until he should be safe, or until he could find means of leaving the country. He had given me his address, which was a good two miles from mine, but in the quieter part of the town, so that I had a hope that no great resistance had been offered there, and that the soldiers would, consequently, be less ferocious than where I lived. In this I was not altogether disappointed. The quarter had been attacked the same day as ours, but there had been few barricades. However, I did not find Torreau at his house. He had not been seen there since early the day before. "You had better look for him at the Hôtel-de-Ville," said his *concierge*, with some irony; and I took his advice to this extent, and I set off towards the Rue de Rivoli. "If I am to find him, chance will help me," I reasoned.

Chance *did* help me. I had not gone half a mile when Torreau came running almost against me down a small slum leading out from a main street. *His hair had turned grey.* In his right hand he held a revolver, and round his waist shone his scarlet sash.

I thought he was flying from pursuers, and exclaimed—"Good God, take that sash off and throw your revolver away. Here, take my arm, quick!"

"No, no, leave me," he cried wildly. "You see what it has come to." (He was gesticulating in a frenzy of exaltation.) "They've butchered, burned, plundered—they, the men of the Commune! They've dishonoured the Republic! France's curse will be upon them for ever—and on me! Let me go, I say! I won't outlive it. Let me go!"

I clung to him as he was bolting; closed with him, and tried to wrench the revolver from his hand. But he resisted with desperation. "Let me go," he shrieked. "Don't be mad!" I cried. "You've a sister and relatives in the world; you've no right to throw away your life. Torreau! Jules! for God's sake, man, have pity on yourself and on me." He sobbed in anguish and resisted the more. I could feel his hot tears dropping on my hands as I forced his arm up, and strove, by exerting all my strength, to make him loosen his hold. "Quick, Torreau! man, I implore you!" I gasped, for the tramping sound of soldiers running at a double, suddenly became audible. He set his teeth and continued to grasp the weapon tighter. I clenched my fist, lifted my arm, and struck him sharply under the elbow. The revolver dropped. But it was too late. A company of cavalry soldiers, with an officer at their head, debouched suddenly on our left, and, in a ringing voice, the officer cried, "Stand!"

The officer was Raoul de Gardefer. He recognized Jules Torreau on the spot, and Torreau recognized him. Of the two, one turned pale, and that one was not Jules Torreau.

The soldiers had already drawn themselves up in a double line, and had loaded their rifles. Raoul de Gardefer would not have saved his former friend if he had gone down on his knees to do it. The soldiers bore carnage in their eyes. Besides, the case was hopeless. Jules' sash was still upon him, and waving his hat above his head, three times he shouted: *"Vive la Commune!"*

This done, he threw his hat, with an appeased look, on the ground, put his back to the wall and crossed his arms on his chest. The soldiers rapped the butt-ends of their rifles on the paving-stones, as if to call on their officer to be quick.

Raoul de Gardefer stepped aside and opened his lips—once, twice—but without speaking. He was ghastly white.

Then Torreau looked at him.

And seeing his lips quiver, something like a flush of emotion stole over Torreau's face; and for the first time since I had known him a faint smile lit up his features.

Lightning Source UK Ltd.
Milton Keynes UK
UKHW010556110219
337000UK00006B/535/P